LOVE CURSED

GODS CURSED SERIES BOOK 1

LEISL LEIGHTON

PERMIEN PRESS

Published by Leisl Leighton as Permien Press. For more information, email: leisl@leislleighton.com

First published 2021 in the A Perfectly Paranormal Valentine Anthology. Rewritten and republished 2022 as a single title novella by Permien Press.

Cover design – Samantha Marshall; Editor – Marnie St Clair

eBook ISBN: 978-0-6451089-5-8; Print ISBN: 978-0-6451089-6-5

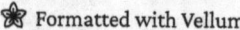 Formatted with Vellum

PRAISE FOR THE GODS CURSED SERIES

Was really hard to put this one down once I started! I can not wait to see what this new series ... Gods Cursed Series.... Holds in the future!

— **DIANA K – GOODREADS & BOOKSPROUT**

Loved this and it's Easter orientated. Check this out.

— **WHITNEY – GOODREADS AND BOOKSPROUT REVIEWER**

"So good! I will always love paranormal romances, they just have so many different types, and themes, and never get boring. Leighton delivers a great one!"

— **TAPNCHICA – GOODREADS AND BOOKSPROUT REVIEWER**

I absolutely love this ... Leighton brilliantly weaves in Greek and Nordic Mythology, Oestra/Easter themes, and a HUGE splash of her rich and thrilling imagination. She is a master at world building, character, plot, and oh...those sex scenes are pretty damn hot. You'd be crazy not to read this series!

— **LAURA BADHUS – GOODREADS REVIEWER**

Loved it !! love this series !! love Korinna and Tamuel.. this is their story... they have history... a fast paced fated mates , second chances, cursed drama... a fast paced action packed drama... so good!!!

— KIMKIM – GOODREADS AND
BOOKSPROUT REVIEWER

This was magical and captivating throughout. Thoroughly enjoyed the storyline and characters and how they overcome things.

— PAT'S REVIEWS - GOODREADS
REVIEWER

I loved this! ... I loved reading about the history and what happened to set things in motion. This is a very good book and is most definitely worth reading.

— A SCHOFIELD - GOODREADS &
BOOKBUB REVIEWER

LOVE CURSED

To my Mum and Dad – you made me believe I could write and get published and let the stories in my heart take shape. Love really can do impossible things.
Thank you.

CHAPTER
ONE

"**W**ould you like a drink, Julianna?"

"Umm ..." Jules blinked rapidly at Simon. Was she supposed to say yes, or no? The information on first dates she'd looked up online hadn't covered this scenario. It was at times like this she really wished she'd inherited her mother's talent for reading minds – although, if she'd inherited her mother's talent, she wouldn't be here. But longing for magic was as useless as longing to have her parents back, so she pushed that thought away as quickly as it had come and tried to read the answer in Simon's eyes.

He began to tap his foot when she didn't answer immediately, then said slowly. "A drink?" His eyes widened a little as he waited for her response.

Did that mean he wanted her to answer yes, or no? Hells, she was so lost.

"Oh, for Goddess-sake! Are you thirsty or not?" the voice in her head snarled.

It was a voice that had come to her on and off all her life, but she'd mostly ignored it. However, something had

1

changed after Christmas and it was now making itself known far more frequently than it ever had before. She had come other think of it as her subconscious rising to the fore as a way to protect herself against increasingly difficult times. She did have a tendency to overthink things and the voice did tend to cut through her overthinking nonsense. She didn't always listen to it, but ...

While it didn't seem particularly happy she was here – it had been very snarky about her date ever since she'd agreed to it – it did have a point right now. Her mouth was incredibly dry, so ... "Yes? Please."

Simon smiled and stood. "Gin and tonic with a twist of lime good for you?"

Yuk. But would he offer that if he didn't think it was the right drink for this situation? Probably not, so ... "Yes please."

A slight nod and another smile.

Another good guess. This was going great even if she did have to drink gin.

"I'll be right back. Make yourself comfortable."

She nodded, even though there was no chance she'd ever be comfortable on this particular sofa. It was over-stuffed, hard and for some strange reason, covered in plastic.

Well, if he truly wanted her comfortable, maybe she didn't have to stay seated.

Jules stood, making a little ripping, sucking sound as the bare part of her legs separated from the plastic – why was it so hot in here? She shouldn't have worn this cream wool dress with its capped sleeves and pretty lace collar. Grandmama always said good wool was cool in summer, warm in winter, but right now, Jules simply found it stifling. However, there was nothing else in her wardrobe that was date worthy.

She quickly sniffed at her armpits, hoping the heat didn't equate to smelly sweat. Thankfully, all she smelled was a faint whiff of her deodorant. Thank the Goddess for that!

Maybe if she walked about a bit, it might help. Waving her hand in front of her face like a fan, she made a little turn around the room. Surely it wasn't rude to look at the artwork and knick-knacks?

She should have done a more thorough job when she'd researched date etiquette. But most of it had been about what date you could first kiss on and what date you could go to second base, who should pay if you went out and so on. Nothing was discussed about a first date where the guy cooked for you at his family home.

It was okay though. She hadn't yet given away that this was the first time she'd been on a date – pitiful given she was 28. Not that she was a virgin – not much better than a virgin, but still, not a virgin. She had some urges and the usual amount of curiosity and it had been easy to assuage that curiosity with a friend at university when she was 20. She couldn't say she had truly enjoyed it, but it had been interesting and she could see that maybe with the right person, it could be pretty special.

Was Simon that someone special? Probably not, but it was something she needed to explore. She owed it to herself to explore it. She truly didn't want to live her life alone. But she hadn't realised how little she knew about dating or being a good date.

Was she being a good date? She was too nervous to know. At least Simon didn't seem to want to chuck her out right away, so that was a good sign. In fact, it seemed like the date was going well.

Date.

Her lips twitched into a smile and, clenching her hands to her chest, she did a little spin on the spot.

She was on a date. An actual date. And her date was making her dinner.

Would he kiss her? She hoped so. Or maybe not. Hells, she didn't know. But it was nice to think there was a chance of something like that happening even if she didn't particularly long for it to happen in the usual tingle-in-the-tummy, curl-the-toes kind of way.

Was that what she would feel if he kissed her? Would it be like kissing that long-ago university friend – something that gave her a little tingle, but more because of the fact it was new rather than creating a great passion. Or would his kiss be more like when Aunt Ophelia kissed her?

The old woman had this thing about kissing on the lips which was a bit odd in a family not given to demonstrative hugging and kissing. But it wasn't even the kissing on the lips that was so bad, it was the fact Aunt O's lips were a curious and shudder-inducing combination of parchment dry yet somehow always sticky. Probably had something to do with the ten-tonne of lipstick she wore. Or the never-ending supply of lollies she munched on.

Thankfully Grandmama had stopped Aunt O from kissing Jules; or touching her as she had a want to do – she was a bit of a close talker – many years ago because her sensitivity to magic had got to the point it was noticeable, and, "We must never let anyone else know of your affliction before we've found the cure!" her grandmama had always lectured.

Jules had always hated that lecture and not simply

4

because it was kind of pointless – it wasn't like she was about to go running around telling everyone about her affliction especially given who her family was and what it could mean if certain people in the community found out. No, she'd hated it because the great Violetta Stevens, Grand Matriarch of the Stevens family and Melbourne Coven Leader, had kept her hope alive for so many years with her talk of a cure.

But there was no cure. No hope. She would always be like this. And if her Grandmama couldn't face the truth of that, well, at least she could, no matter how much it hurt.

And, if she were to look on the bright side, Grandmama's protectiveness and the affliction had saved her from Aunt O's kisses, so, it wasn't all bad.

Although, right now, given nobody but Bas had touched her for years, she almost missed Aunt O's disgusting kisses.

Hells. She did want Simon to kiss her, if only for the aching need inside her to be assuaged. And if anyone could do it, it should be him. She hadn't had any unfortunate reactions to being in this room with him for the ten minutes they had sat chatting – well, he chatted and she listened. He did seem to love talking about his work; and she had to admit it was interesting hearing about the potions he created with the little bit of magic he had access to. Not that he'd put it like that. He'd made it sound like his magic was grand, but she knew better. She wouldn't be here if it was.

But that was by-the-by. Hearing about the kind of magical work he did filled in some gaps she didn't know she had in her knowledge base. The books and grimoires she worked with and catalogued in the Coven Library under Stevens House didn't mention small household spells like the ones he seemed so proud of.

But the best thing was, that even though he spoke about magic, and she'd known coming here that he had access to very little, there didn't seem to be any around him at all. She hadn't even felt a tingle from him when he'd sat on the couch right next to her after taking her cardigan. She also hadn't felt a tingle of anything else looking into his handsome face with his hair slicked back like some mobster from the twenties and a superior smile twitching on his lips as he bragged about his latest stain-removal feat.

Probably not a great sign given this was a date, but beggars couldn't be choosers.

The Council would never countenance her dating anyone outside of the magical community – they didn't know about the university friend – but given her affliction, she couldn't date anyone inside of it, so she'd always been stuck. But after hearing Grandmama complain about him and his family and their ebbing magical abilities and how the rest of the Council were on a mission to oust families that were not pulling their weight, she knew this could be her chance.

She might not want another date with Simon – especially if he kept looking at her as he'd done when she'd arrived, like he was about to win a prize. He had no idea she was no prize despite her family name and their standing in the magical community – but she wasn't about to explain that to him. It certainly wouldn't be a tick in the right column at this early stage.

"Here you go, my dear. Let me know if it's too strong."

She took the proffered drink and sipped obediently, trying very hard not to gag as the horrid taste of juniper and alcohol filled her mouth. Thankfully, he'd made a very weak gin and tonic, so she was able to swallow it and not spray the mouthful all over his beautifully pressed suit. "It's love-ly," she said, smiling up at him.

"You know, gin is what prostitutes used to drink. It was cheap and rotted their brains, so their job was at least bearable."

She widened her smile, trying to ignore the voice in her head. It was particularly acerbic today. When it was like this is was difficult to accept it was her subconscious. Maybe she had multiple personalities. Perhaps her the increasing seriousness of her affliction was also driving her insane.

"You're saner than he is. Do you think he thinks looking at you like that is charming?"

Oh Goddess. Simon *was* looking at her funny. Did she have a maniacal grin on her face? She pressed her lips together and looked away, her gaze lighting on the humon-gous and ugly portrait that hung over the mantlepiece. "This is ... astonishing."

Simon's gaze immediately swung to the portrait. "Yes, isn't it? We're very proud of it. Mother commissioned the portrait a few years ago and Armando Sinclair himself came to do the drawings. He's a 'normal' but is very talented."

She nodded knowingly even though she had no idea who Armando Sinclair was – obviously someone well-known in stuffy circles going by the expression on Simon's face and his air of general satisfaction as he gestured at the portrait. "It's very ... lifelike. I almost feel like your mother's eyes are following me." She hid a shudder.

"Yes, it's a feature of Armando's work. He likes to draw the viewer into the painting. See how the smile on her face almost says, 'come to me'."

"More like 'run far away, little peasant'."

Jules choked back the urge to laugh as she said to the voice in her mind, *"Not now, please. You can talk as much as you like later. Just not now. I don't want to ruin this. If things go well, I'll have a date on Valentine's Day. I might not ever get another chance."*

An aggravated sigh was her only answer.

"Thank you."

"You won't thank me if you stay much longer with this pillock."

She clapped her hand against her mouth to stop the snort of laughter from erupting.

"Julianna? Are you okay?"

"I'm fine. Drink just went down the wrong way."

He frowned at her. "Perhaps I did make it a little strong. Here, let me fix it."

He took the drink from her – she hoped by some miracle he might not bring it back – then just as he went to turn, a bell sounded from the next room.

"Ah, our dinner is ready. Let me show you to the table and I'll fetch it for us."

She allowed him to take her elbow and lead her into a formal and very stuffy blue and gold dining room – Goddess! Did they think they were living at the Palace at Versailles? – and then stood as he pulled out a chair at one end of the table.

"Sit here and I will be right back with our Pasta al tomato and our Salad al Verde."

"What language does he think he's parroting?"

Jules held onto her snort only as long as it took the door to slap shut behind Simon.

"He's an idiot," the voice said.

"Be nice."

"Hard to in the face of such idiocy. You can't seriously consider going on another date with him?"

"Maybe."

"Well, then, you'd be the idiot. Especially given the fact you have someone so much better waiting in the wings."

Jules snorted. *"If that were true, I wouldn't be here."*

"If only you could see. He's waiting there for both of us. He's —" The voice cut off with a choking sound as pain, sharp and icy, spiked through her head.

"Ow!" she gasped, clutching at her head as the kitchen door swung open and Simon entered with a tray covered with a large and very shiny metal cloche.

"Ta-da. Our dinner is served." Thankfully he was too busy looking at the cloche to notice she was in pain.

She quickly dropped her hands and said, "Yummy," trying her best to cover the fact her eyelid still twitched from the pain echoing through her head. Perhaps she should go and get her head scanned – these attacks were getting worse and worse.

"It won't help," the voice said, the sound of it not much more than a whimper.

"Shut up and go away."

"I beg your pardon?" Simon had stopped a few feet away from the table, his handsome face marred by outraged surprise.

Damn it. Had she said that out loud? "Sorry," she said quickly. "I was talking about my phone. I must have left it on in my handbag in the other room."

"Your phone? I can't hear it ringing."

"Oh, can't you. Well, that's good then. Shall I help you with this?" she said, standing so abruptly she knocked the chair over.

"Careful!" Simon shouted as she made a grab for it, catching it before it hit the floor. "Mama would be extremely annoyed if those chairs were damaged. She hunted for months for just the right shade of blue in the tapestry and just the right honey in the wood and ended up getting them shipped from a monastery high in the Austrian Alps. They are very expensive."

She gingerly put it back in place. "If they are so expensive, should we even eat in here?"

"Of course. Where else would I entertain Julianna Stevens, granddaughter of our Coven Leader?"

"Where else indeed. And please, it's Jules."

"Really?" His tone and the tightening of his mouth suggested what he really meant was 'It's so ... common'. But to his credit, he rallied, and with a nod to her seat, said, "Sit please ... Jules. Let me serve you then we can chat and get to know each other better."

She sat back in the chair very carefully and waited as Simon served the pasta – tomato and basil from the smell. He grated parmesan over it without asking her if she wanted any – she did, but twice the meagre amount he'd put on – placing it down in front of her with a flourish. He then served her a small plate of salad – a few lettuce leaves with a few pieces of tomato and basil and way too much balsamic dressing from the smell and the drenched look of the leaves – and then, after serving himself, took a seat at the other end of the twelve-seater table.

"Bon appetito," he said and tucked in.

"*Idiot,*" the voice muttered, making her snort just as she lifted her first mouthful to her lips. A piece of tomato-soaked pasta dropped from the fork, hit her breast and ran a snail-trail down the front of her cream dress.

"Damn," she muttered.

"Oh, you are a klutz," Simon said. "But here, let me fix that for you. I've been working on a new cleaning spell for just this occasion."

"No, don't—"

But it was too late, he'd released the small spell. It hit her square in the chest, fizzed around her for a moment as if it wasn't going to work and then,

BANG!

Her allergy to magic reacted forcibly. The table in front of her blew up and she was thrown back by the force of the explosion, tomato pasta and salad flying everywhere. She hit the wall with a loud smack of breaking plaster, wood and crockery. Her head hurt from where it had impacted with the wall, but that pulse of pain wasn't as bad as the smarting cuts that sliced her skin everywhere the magic touched her or the nausea roiling in her stomach. She slid down the wall and fell onto her hands and knees, heaving everything she'd eaten in the last half day onto the floor. Somewhere in her mind she was conscious of a voice screaming obscenities.

Despite the pain sparking through her and the fact every movement threatened more vomiting, she managed to look up and across the room.

Simon was trying to extricate himself from a tangle of broken chairs while swearing and screaming like a banshee.

Shit. Had she done that? She had to get over there, apologise, make certain he wasn't so angry he'd do something she really didn't want him to do. Something that would make Grandmama very angry. She pushed groggily to her feet and staggered over to him, somehow managing not to vomit again. "Sorry. So sorry. I didn't mean to ... I can't help it ..." She managed to help him get free of the chairs.

Simon rolled to his side, pushed to his feet and staggered away from her. "That was you?"

"Yes. In part. I'm allergic to magic," she blurted out.

"You ... what? You're magically disabled?"

"Oops. Cat's out of the bag now. Too bad, so sad."

11

But she barely heard the voice in her head because Simon was looking at her like she was some kind of monster. "A witch who is allergic to magic? Why … Your family should never let you out of the house! It's criminal. I would never have … look at what you've done!"

Face hot with her anger and chest heaving, she couldn't stop herself from saying, "It was partly your fault. You shouldn't use magic on others without first asking permission."

"I … You …" His mouth opened and closed like a guppy, bits of pasta and tomato falling from his head as he shook his fist at her. "It wouldn't have been a problem if you weren't an abomination. Get out! Get out of my house. I will be seeking reparations from your grandmother, that I promise you. You haven't heard the end of this!"

There were things she should have said to him – he was being very rude when it was half his fault – but what was the point? She wouldn't win him over despite her previous thoughts. And after Grandmama got over her anger, she would cover this up by fixing the damages and wiping memories. She only wished Violetta could wipe her memory because she'd love to forget this disaster. And the dream she'd had that for this once, she wouldn't be alone and loveless on Valentine's Day.

Jules turned, shoulders slumped, arms wrapped around herself. She should have known better than to try for something close to normal.

She grabbed her bag from the other room, limped out the front door and only hoped she wouldn't bump into anyone she knew before she could get home and out of her tomato, basil and blood-soaked dress and have a shower. It was going to be embarrassing enough having to explain this to her grandmama without having to deal with anyone else seeing her as well.

And Bas wouldn't be pleased.

She sighed. She'd have to avoid him until morning when he was back in his cat form. Pity. She could do with one of his hugs right about now but that would have to wait until tomorrow night when he was in his human form again and she'd made certain he wouldn't go after Simon.

Her lip wobbled and she swiped at the tears that fell down her cheeks. Why did her life have to be so complicated and difficult?

Thankfully, the voice remained silent. Good. She really couldn't deal with it right now.

TWO

"Bastien? Where are you?"

"Shh." He poked his head out of his room to wave Tamuel, his cupid 'brother', in from the hallway. Despite being blind in his human form, he could still see the cupid's aura shining in the darkness of the hallway due to the enormous power he held, jewel bright with greens and purples and yellows and vibrating outwards. "Tighten your hold on your powers. Jules is asleep in the room next door."

"At this hour?"

"She went to bed early with a headache. I don't want to wake her."

"No. I imagine you don't."

He nodded at his old friend. There was no way Jules could know what they were up to. Too much was at stake if they wanted this to work.

And he needed it to work. He'd lived without hope for so long. The unbinding of the curse that had made his life a living hell for 2,000 years had seemed nothing but a pipe dream for so long.

A pipe dream tied to a small loophole once every 200 years on Valentine's Day Eve.

A loophole that had seemed beyond his grasp when one after another reincarnation of Julianna Stevius – Lianna to everyone who had known her back then – barely acknowledged he was alive, let alone had the curiosity to question the nightmares they endured and the fact they reacted badly to magic. They'd just ... accepted, Lianna's spirit pushed so far down inside them by the curse that he could do nothing about the silent screaming he sometimes thought he heard from her.

But Jules was different from all who came before, and her birth and the fact Tamuel had finally found the journal had—

"Where do you want me to drop the boxes?" Tamuel asked.

"In the library—no! Don't use your magic here. You'll hurt Jules – I can't believe you'd forget."

"I didn't forget. But she's not in this room – you never said she had become *that* sensitive."

Bastien shrugged. Violetta could barely even touch her granddaughter now for fear of Jules' magical sensitivity reacting to the power just under her skin. He never thought he'd be grateful the curse had taken all but a smidgeon of his power – and in the last year or so, it had taken nearly all of what he had left – but at least it allowed him to touch her. She was rarely ever touched by anyone anymore. "I thought I'd mentioned to you that it's been getting worse lately. Much worse."

"A sign?"

He shrugged again. Tamuel's guess was as good as his. "We also don't want Violetta sensing you were here when she gets back. She's not expecting you to arrive with the shipment of ancient books and manuscripts until next week – you're supposed to be stuck in Rome." Tamuel's well-constructed role of magical artefacts dealer, Tomaso di Erosi, alongside a friendship he'd struck up with Violetta and her deceased husband many years ago, had helped as a cover for why he was around so much, but it wouldn't explain why he was here now at this hour or why he had the journal they needed Jules to 'find'.

"Here – take my arm. I'll lead you downstairs," Tamuel said.

Bastien brushed his friend's arm aside, trying very hard not to be annoyed, but the cupid should know better than to treat him like an invalid. Especially after all this time. But sometimes he slipped. Bastien put it down to his cupid need to please – and that was the only reason he held his temper as he said, "I might be blind in this form, but I know my way around this house and the library better than you – I have lived here ever since Tamara Stevens built it 150 years ago."

"Of course. Sorry. You are right. Lead the way."

He made his way out into the hall, down the stairs, across the foyer to the door that led to the library that lay in the secret underground caverns deep below Stevens House. He led Tamuel down the four flights of stairs, their foot-steps echoing off the stone walls and arched ceiling. The sound changed as they stepped into the huge library at the end of the stairs, disappearing in the high arches of wood and stone overhead and the stacks that filled the cavernous space and multiple specialised rooms that made up the library.

He didn't bother to turn on the lights in the massive chandeliers overhead. He certainly didn't need the light to get around and Tamuel had the eyesight of a cupid so didn't even need to use his magic to light his way.

As he moved into the library, there came a rustling from the far corners and a rushing pressure – the ghosts of Stevens House coming out to protect what was theirs from intruders. "It's just me and Tamuel," he said. They immediately settled down and went back to whatever they did when they weren't haunting someone or protecting the library.

"So it's safe to teleport the boxes in now?" Tamuel said, pulling Bastien's attention back to the job at hand.

"Yes. There's enough stone and dirt between us. Jules won't be affected. And any leftover magic will be syphoned into the magical ark that Violetta created recently to protect Jules from the latent magic in many of the books, so she can continue to work down here. So neither of them will sense you used any magic down here even if they came down in half an hour."

"Clever." There was a light thump as the load of boxes filled with old books, journals and manuscripts landed at the base of the steps. Good. Jules wouldn't miss them there. "What now?"

"Unpack half of the top box and put the books on the kitchen table in a pile with the journal on the top."

"The kitchen table?"

Bastien nodded. "Jules won't be able to ignore them. And when she sees the age of the journal, she won't be able to stop herself from reading it before she does anything else."

"Are you certain?"

Bastien raised his brow. "Does a cat love cream?"

"I don't know – do you?"

"Ha." He didn't bother mentioning that when forced

17

into his cat body during the day, he no longer touched dairy – it made him feel a little ill now like it would a real cat. Not a good sign at all.

"Here, hold the journal while I take care of the rest."

Tamuel pushed an old leather-bound manuscript into his hands – Jules would be horrified neither of them were wearing cotton gloves to handle it. Even so, his fingers tightened around the soft leather binding. "Hello, old friend."

He couldn't believe he was finally holding it. It had taken so long to track it down, and when Tamuel had told him this last Christmas that he had a lead he knew would allow them to find it, Bas had tried to stop his expectations from soaring – they'd had so many leads that had gone nowhere over the years. But still he'd hoped more than he'd ever hoped before because this had truly felt like their last chance.

And now he was holding it in his hands.

He'd spent many hours watching Esta write this journal, listening to her ponder what to put into it about the curse and what had happened to him and Lianna. It was meant to be a bridge between him and the Stevius family after she'd gone, to explain the curse – a curse that cruelly stopped him from talking about it and what had happened – and to ask for help in finding a way to break it.

But this journal was more than that. It was a history of his and Lianna's love.

Esta had written about how he and Lianna had met, how it had been love at first sight, how, despite Lianna's vows and his job as a cupid, neither of them had been able to do anything but give in to their desires. With one meeting of gazes in that crowded marketplace, he'd known she was his soulmate and they were destined for each other.

A fact that had made him the happiest cupid alive.

Until Clodia had used it against them to curse them.

If not for Esta, he would have lost himself to madness. But Esta had come back in secret after the dust had settled and found him, taking him to her family. Even so young, she'd had the power to bind him to her sister to keep him safe. The only thing she couldn't tell him was what had happened to his son. She went back to serve out her time with the Vestal Virgins, always on the lookout for information about the baby, but never found anything.

He assumed the baby was either found by someone – maybe Eros given the baby would have been born a cupid and he would have been drawn to it by the cupid powers – or had died in the explosion of power, his soul and body mercifully taken to the heavens. Eros of course had studiously ignored him since he was cursed so he could never find out if his father had indeed taken his grandson under his wing. In regard to the latter ... well, he tried very hard not to think about it, but of late it had snuck in more and more often as the most probable explanation for what had happened to the newborn baby.

Either way, the loss of his son was an eternal grief, one that the years had only dulled not made disappear.

Maybe now he had the diary and breaking the curse was closer than it had ever been, he'd be able to find out. But first, they had to break the curse.

His fingers curled around the journal even more tightly. They had so much riding on it. And if it did what they hoped it would, he would finally be able to truly pay Esta back for all she'd done for him.

Years after that horrible night of death and loss, when

Esta had finally been released from her 30 years of service, he'd thanked her for all she'd done by vowing to always be a guardian to her and her family. Not a selfless vow given he wanted to be close when Lianna was reborn into her family line as all witches were every few hundred years.

Unfortunately, knowledge of why he was cursed, and how he came to be bonded to the Stevius family, died with Esta's great-great-granddaughter when the journal he now held in his hand was lost in a house fire – or so he'd thought. Hope had died, little by little with every century that passed and nobody questioned what forced him to live as a cat by day, blind man by night or why he was struck down with extreme pain if he ever tried to talk about any of it. Pain that only got worse if he ever tried to be more than a guardian towards Lianna's reincarnations.

Life had become monotonous and hopeless until Tamuel found him a century ago and told him he wanted to help. He would never have thought a fellow cupid had it in them to care about anything other than their job, but Tamuel had proved to be different.

He'd said that all curses were a horrifying cruelty, a wrong that needed to be righted if they could. Not only that, but he'd also had much to say about how wrong it was that Eros had never tried to break the curse binding his son – and one of the greatest cupids of his time – keeping him from his soulmate. He also thought it was his job, as a cupid, to put two lovers back together who should never have been parted.

It had given Bastien hope; hope that had grown with Jules' birth. It was like Lianna was more alive in her than ever before. And somehow, he was more than a guardian to her. They were best friends.

It would be different this time. It had to be.

He took in a deep breath. "This is going to work," he said to Tamuel.

Tamuel put his arm around Bastien's shoulder. "Yes, it is. I'm certain of it. It's long past time this curse was ended."

Bastien swallowed hard. "Yes, it is."

Tamuel squeezed his shoulder and then turned back to his task. A few moments later, he asked, "Does it matter where on the table I put these?"

"No. Anywhere will get her attention. She has this thing about books and food—" He whipped around at a sound coming from upstairs, his hand going out to slap against Tamuel's chest. "Did you hear that?"

"What?"

There was another shuffling thunk and a curse. "That. Jules. She's moving around upstairs."

"How can you tell it's her? I can barely hear anything."

"She just swore under her breath."

"You really do have the hearing of a cat."

"Can you finish up down here without me?"

"I think I can manage such a difficult task by myself," Tamuel said.

Bastien ignored the sarcasm and ran to the stairs.

"Wait!" Tamuel called out.

He stopped. "Shh. She'll hear you."

"Sorry."

"Well? What did you stop me for?" He really needed to get upstairs. Jules sounded like she was limping. And was that blood he could smell? And tomatoes? What the hell?

"The journal." The flaring movement of the cupid's aura showed Bastien that Tamuel held out his hand, pointing to the book clutched against Bastien's chest.

He couldn't believe he'd forgotten he held it. It would

21

have been a disaster if Jules had seen it in his arms. The curse would never let him hand over such essential information to her so easily. As it was, even helping Tamuel to set up the journal for Jules to find caused a burning sensation in his chest that wasn't exactly pleasant. "Here." He put the journal down on top of the boxes Tamuel had magicked in minutes ago then took the stairs two at a time.

He burst out of the stairwell into the foyer and stopped.

Jules wasn't in the foyer – there was no sign of her blue and green aura with its dark heart of amethyst glowing in the cavernous space. But she was close. Her presence called to him like a beacon, especially when something was wrong.

And there definitely was something wrong.

CHAPTER
THREE

The scent of blood and tomatoes – and basil – mingled with the scent of vanilla and cinnamon that was purely Jules. It led towards the back of the house; not upstairs like he'd expected.

He moved quickly down the arched hallway, his feet padding softly on the polished floorboards. He followed the scent into the kitchen, circling around the large island bench and past the table, heading towards the laundry – and cursed when he tripped over something on the floor.

A handbag by the feel of it. Strange. Jules had been brought up to always be neat and tidy so that the map of the house in Bastien's head wasn't disturbed by anything being out of place. The fact she'd just dropped her bag in the middle of the floor wasn't good. Also, why would she need a handbag if she'd just come down to the kitchen from her room to get something to eat? Had she been out without telling him?

His worry spiked. He picked the bag up and put it on the table, his hand coming away wet. He lifted it to his nose – tomatoes, basil and a hint of blood. "What the hell?"

"Hello?" Jules's voice wavered out of the laundry. "Is that you, Bastien?"

"Yes." He was long past being surprised that she could sense him in the same way he sensed her – another difference with this incarnation. "What's happened? What are you doing down here? You went to bed with a headache. I thought you were asleep."

"I spilled something on myself." Her voice was muffled then became clear. "I'm just putting it in the washing machine. You head up to bed. I can deal with this."

He got to the door just as the washing machine started up.

"If you spilled something, why can I smell blood?" He stopped in the doorway, taken aback by her aura – it was unsettled, vibrating wildly, colours flashing randomly as if she'd been shocked. That only happened when she was exposed to magic. "Jules. What the fuck happened?"

"Shh," she said, rushing towards him, her aura pulsing faster and incredibly bright – so bright he could see the entire outline of her body, including the wild mass of her curling dark auburn hair that swung down her back rather than being caught in the tight bun she usually favoured. "Stop shouting. I don't want Violetta to wake up."

"Your grandmama is out."

"Bugger I really need her to—"

The way she stopped abruptly made his hackles rise further. "What happened?"

"I don't want to say right now."

"Why not?"

"Because ..." She flapped her hands around, the movement clearly visible inside her aura. "Because ..." He knew her well enough to know she was trying desperately to think of something to tell him that wouldn't make him a)

24

worried; b) get angry; or c) get her into trouble with her grandmama. Given she wanted to talk to Violetta, it was obviously either a or b. Probably both.

Sighing, he said, "Jules. You know I can see your aura, right?"

She slouched and made a squished sound of frustration. "Can explanations wait until after I've had a shower? I'm covered in pasta sauce—"

"And blood."

"And blood," she groaned. "You know, it's not fair you still have the senses of a cat even when you're in your human form."

"It makes up for the blindness."

She swore under her breath and touched his arm. "I'm sorry. That was mean of me. It's just—"

"You're in pain."

"Yes. And I wish you hadn't caught me like this."

She gestured again and he thought at first she meant covered in pasta sauce and blood, but then realised she must be standing there in only her underwear because she'd put her clothes into the washing machine. Swallowing hard against the familiar but inconvenient desire that surged through him, he said roughly, "Right. Shower and change, then explanations."

"If you insist."

"I do."

"Okay. But please, promise you won't lecture me. I already know what I did was stupid."

He snorted. "I'll try."

He followed her upstairs and sat on the edge of her bed as she disappeared into the ensuite with her pyjamas. He wished now he hadn't insisted on moving his bed to the room next door years ago. He'd been happy to be there for her when she was young, but as she grew into adulthood, it was too hard. Courtesy of the curse, she just couldn't see him as anything other than a friend, and it was a constant ache, especially at night when he lay awake keeping watch over her as she slept.

He'd asked Violetta to make up some lore about him that said he must sleep elsewhere when his witch reached a certain age, and thankfully, Jules had swallowed it. Even so, there were times that he did stay in here with her. Especially when the nightmares made her scream and cry. Nightmares she could never remember once she woke but that he knew were memories of the last few months of Lianna's life and death. Those nights, when he came in to hold her and stay with her to help her fall back to sleep were both the best and worst nights of his life. So close, and yet so horribly far away from what he knew they could be.

Given all that, it was absurd that sitting here now while she showered felt too intimate.

He shifted to the floor.

After ten minutes, the bathroom door opened, a cloud of steamy air billowed out into the room – he could feel the humidity of it covering him. With it came the scent of vanilla and cinnamon – and a little citrus tonight. And underneath it all, the faint smell of blood. She'd obviously been exposed to magic. But how? The magic Tamuel had used would have been shielded by the layers of rock and soil between the house and the library, so that couldn't be it. "How badly did the magic lash you? Do you need to be bandaged up?"

"No. The cuts aren't bad."

"Cuts?"

She sighed and sat on the bed beside him, crossing her

legs to face him. "I wasn't asleep in bed like you thought. I lied about the headache."

"Why?"

"I had a date."

"What?" The pain of that statement jagged through him, but he swallowed it down. "Who? Did you go to a magic club? Is that why you were bleeding? You know this is exactly why you can't go out with anyone in our community—"

"Whoa – you promised no lectures."

"Sorry – it's just … I didn't expect you to do something like this."

"What? Try to be happy? Try to find love?" She sighed, her aura sparking around her in agitation. "I'm lonely, Bastien. The only friends I have in my life are you and Grandmama and while I treasure both of you in my life, it's …"

"Not enough."

"Yes."

Oh Gods. If she only knew he was her soulmate, the one who loved her best in the world and that she loved him; was meant for him. But he couldn't tell her. Even thinking of it made pain stab through his head. He hid the pain and reached out for her hands, holding them gently in his even though touching her always brought with it an ache of loss – his loss, her loss – and a simmering anger he'd never been able to put aside.

Fuck Clodia and her curse. If he ever got his hands on her, he would do worse than kill her, he would … He sighed internally. It was useless to rage about what he would do because he could do nothing – even if she wasn't long dead, his powers were bound by the curse.

Hopefully, once Jules found the journal he and Tamuel

had planted, and read what was inside, she'd remember what she needed to do to break this curse. But he couldn't tell her any of it. All he could do was be here in whatever way she needed – and right now, she needed her friend. So, he swallowed the pain and asked, "Who is he?"

"Simon Smithson-West."

"Smithson-West? The cleaning specialist family Violetta was going on about last week because their magic is waning?"

"Yes. His magic is particularly weak so I thought he would be safe."

"Jules, you know better than that. No magic is safe."

"What am I supposed to do? Go out with a human?"

"Of course not." It was against their laws. Humans couldn't be trusted with knowledge of their world – too many bad things had happened in the past when they became aware magical people and creatures lived among them. Not to mention the thought of her going out with anyone but him was a stab to his heart.

"So, I'm just ... what? Meant to live alone forever?"

"Jules." He pulled her forward and she tumbled against him, her arms going around him, holding tight. "I didn't mean—"

Jules shook her head against his chest. "No. Don't worry about it. It's not your fault I'm an abomination."

He stiffened. "Abomination?" He pulled away, wishing to all the Gods he could see her face because her voice was expressionless. "Who told you that? Simon?"

"He was angry—"

"That doesn't excuse him calling you that or using his magic on you." Of course that's what had happened – nothing else explained the blood and pasta sauce that had been all over her. "I'm going to kill him."

28

"No." She gripped his arms as if she really thought he was about to go and follow through on his words. "He's not worth it. Besides, he got punished enough with the backlash. It ruined his entire dining room." She snickered. "He'll be using his powers to clean that room for the next few weeks."

"Good." It wasn't enough. Not nearly enough. But there wasn't really anything he could do. It wasn't like he could realistically go around to the warlock's house to teach him a lesson – he couldn't go anywhere without a Stevens, tied to their bloodline like he was. And Jules would hardly drive him over there so he could castrate the bastard as he deserved. Abomination! He deserved more than castration, the donkey's arse!

"Why did he use his powers on you?" It wasn't something a powered person would usually do without permission – certainly not on someone from their community. The ramifications of doing so had caused blood feuds between families in the past, exposing them to humans – which was why it was pretty much outlawed to use magic on anyone without permission.

Jules sighed. "We were having dinner at his house – he cooked tomato and basil pasta. I dropped some on my cream dress and he offered to use his latest cleaning spell to fix the stain."

"He did more than offer."

"Yes, well, it's apparently a specialty of his and he was pretty enthusiastic and wanted to help and let the spell go before I could stop him." She screwed her mouth to the side again. "If you think about it, it was kind of gentlemanly."

Bastien snorted. "Even if that were true, from the sounds of it, he wasn't gentlemanly afterwards."

"Well, it's kind of understandable. The backlash that

destroyed his dining room threw him across the room. He was hurt and upset, even more so when I blurted out my apologies and accidentally told him about my magical allergy. He ... lost his shit."

"Jules." He wanted to pull her back into his arms but she sat stiffly, holding herself apart – holding herself together? He could see in her aura the hurt she felt. He sidled closer and began to rub her back as she always liked, but she winced and he quickly stopped. "Sorry."

She grabbed his hand, pulled it back towards her. "No, don't stop. That felt nice."

"But you're hurt." It must have been bad for the backlash to have caused cuts on her back too.

"I'm fine. Just paper-cuts really. They'll heal in a few days. Just hold me until I fall asleep. Please?"

He did just that, lying down so she could cuddle into his side, and stroked her hair. He hoped she'd fall asleep well before sunrise when he'd need to leave her before the change took him over. She must have been tired because her breathing slowed within minutes, the tension easing out of her body as she fell asleep.

Soon, he'd be able to do this every night.

She'd find the journal tomorrow and read it and then she'd know she was cursed, would know he was tied up in that curse too, and she'd want to break it. And even though it was cutting it close, with only thirteen days until Valentine's Eve, he knew she could do it.

Not that there was any other choice – they couldn't have given her more warning than this or the curse could try to stop them. It had proved to be just that insidious over the years.

Thirteen days until they were both free.

Thirteen days until he could tell her everything he'd

held inside for too long and share with her what had been stolen from them almost two millennia ago. For too long, Valentine's Day had signified a happy never after for them. But this year, he was certain it would be the first day of happy ever afters from here-on out.

It had to be.

FOUR

J ules yawned widely as she made her way down the stairs, Bastien in cat form trotting beside her.

She was so tired. Even though she'd slept well until Bastien had left her this morning, she'd fallen into the horror of the nightmares after he had left. As always, they left her feeling exhausted after waking from them, as if she had truly suffered the trauma of them.

She shuddered just thinking about them. In fact, she would prefer not to think of them. They sucked all the life and light out of a room.

Hang on. That wasn't a metaphor. There literally was no light around her. None of the sconces of the walls were lit.

She'd been so tired she hadn't noticed as she'd rounded the corner and continued down the stairs. So far down no light shone from above.

And no light was coming from below like it usually would. The stairwell was in complete, stygian darkness.

Her foggy mind startled into instant alert.

Her breath, a heavy pant, echoed off the grey stone

walls as she tried to swallow down rising panic, caught statue-like between one step and the next.

Don't be silly. It's just a stupid childhood fear.

"No it's not. No it's not. The nightmare's real. We're being buried alive."

She clutched her throat. *"Stop it. Stop it. That's not happening. It's not real."*

"But the dark! We hate the dark."

"Shut up. Just shut up and stop panicking and we'll be okay." Stupid internal voice! If it wasn't being sarcastic and unhelpful, it was filling her with unreasoning panic.

That was mostly when it had come to her in the past - when she was in any dark or enclosed spaces. She'd been unable to sleep with the light off at all when she was a child primarily because of the fear the voice filled her with about the darkness.

It was so stupid. She was an adult now. Childish fears caused by her subconscious voice shouldn't cause this amount of panic. But it did. Every time.

She tried to grip a hold of her common sense. She was one flight from the bottom so it made more sense to continue down than flee back up the stairwell. There was light to be had at the bottom of the steps just one turn in the stairwell and then a few steps away from the last stair. A switch. On the wall. She just needed to reach it. That's all.

All she needed to do to get there and turn it on was take one step at a time.

And breathe. Breathing would be good.

She took a big breath. Then a step. Then another.

Her grandmama had obviously forgotten to turn on the lights when she came down earlier to do the magical part of her research before Jules started her hours in the library. She was usually so good about turning the lights on, even though she could use her witch lighting to light her way and didn't need the electric lights like Jules did. Violetta must have been super pre-occupied to have forgotten.

"Use the torch on your phone."

"I forgot to charge it last night. It's still in my bag in the kitchen."

"Oh, Goddess. Did the ceiling just move down a bit?"

"Shut up."

She really needed to do something about her internal voice. Only crazy people talked to themselves as if their internal voice was a different person. Oh Goddess. The thought she'd had last night at Simon's might actually be true. She was going crazy.

"You're crazy to be walking into that darkness."

She ignored the voice's negativity and reached out, only a little relieved to feel the cold stone under her palm. She pictured the arcs of stone and wood that made up the ceiling. How high and solid they were, how when the lights – in the sconces on the walls and in the chandeliers – were on, the underground space felt airy and spacious despite the crowded stacks.

Keeping her hand on the wall, she carefully made her way down into the Coven library.

She loved the library.

"When it's lit."

She shuddered and made herself think about the work she so loved: working with her grandmama, upholding their family's grand tradition as keepers of the greatest works of magic in the southern hemisphere.

As she took the turn into the last stretch of steps, there came a rustle and whispering from the dark cavernous space below.

"What's that? Is the roof caving in?"

She swallowed hard. "*No.*"

"*Are we sure it's not the ceiling caving in?*"

"*Absolutely. You know it's just the family ghosts. They're harmless.*"

"*That's what you think. Ghosts are never harmless.*"

"*Well, they've never hurt me.*"

Bastien chose that moment to rub against her leg. She jumped, shrieking, the sound echoing in the stone stairwell around her.

"Meow?"

His worry was clear and she felt bad for causing such a scene. She knew he was there and shouldn't have been so shocked when he tried to comfort her. She'd been so wound up though. Which of course was why he had tried to comfort her.

Stupid. So stupid.

"Meow?" His query as he rubbed up against her leg again, as if asking if she was okay, made her smile.

"I'm okay," she said. She couldn't see him, his black fur at one with the darkness surrounding her, but then he looked up, his peridot-coloured eyes a bright glow in the dark. Seeing them helped her fear retreat a little. She smiled. "I'm okay, I promise," she repeated. "You go and turn the kettle on for me while I find the light."

He made a meeping sound and took off, taking his night-glow eyes with him.

"*That was a mistake.*"

"*No. I can do this.*" Just two more steps to the library floor, a few paces along the wall towards the kitchen to reach the light switch and ...

"Yaahhh!" She tripped over, pitching forward to land smack on something that crumpled under her weight but had sharp edges that dug into her leg and side. "What the ever-loving—"

"Julianna dear, are you okay?" Her grandmama's voice came from deep within the stacks.

"I'm fine."

"Sorry, I forgot to turn the lights on. Be careful of the boxes at the bottom of the steps. We had a delivery from Tomaso last night and I haven't had a chance to move them."

"Right. Thanks."

"Could have had that warning 30 seconds ago!"

She pushed upright from where she'd landed on top of a box, rubbing her jeans-clad thigh where a bruise was likely blooming. Oh well, it would just add to the pinprick bruises she had all over her torso from last night's magical explosion.

"We promised Bastien we weren't going to think about that idiot again."

"Yeah, I'm trying not to."

"Try harder. Remember that he called you an abomination and magically disabled."

"He wasn't wrong."

"Coming from someone whose claim to fame is stain-removal spells ... really!"

"Yeah. But ... I'd so hoped to have a date for Valentine's Day finally."

"That won't happen until we overcome the curse – ow!"

She winced and rubbed her forehead wondering over her internal voice's use of the word 'curse'. A Freudian slip? Had she subconsciously realised something her conscious hadn't?

Nah.

There was no way she was cursed – even though it

would certainly explain a thing or two about her life. But it was ridiculous. Who would bother cursing her?

Not that she wanted to be cursed. Poor Bastien went through hell twice every 24 hours because of the curse that had been placed on him by some mysterious witch many centuries ago before he'd been taken in by her long-dead ancestor.

Of course, the only reason they knew he was cursed was because curses were Violetta's research specialty. Nobody in the family had ever questioned what made Bastien turn into a cat during the day or why he was bonded to their family. He was just a family fixture. But Violetta had figured it out when she was in her teens and had worked since then trying to learn everything she could about curses to help him.

So far, she'd discovered a curse could only be removed in three ways according to the lore – by the original castor; by finding a loophole within the original casting (there were often loopholes, according to Violetta); or by discovering where the spell was cast and casting a spell that was its equal yet opposite on a significant anniversary of the original casting.

Apart from that, all information about Bastien's curse remained elusive and the curse itself made it impossible for him to talk about the details.

But if anyone could find a way, Violetta would. Jules was certain of it.

She wished she could be the one to help him. More than wished it. Every part of her ached with the need to do something to ease his torment and find a solution. That need had grown since Christmas for some reason she couldn't explain other than he seemed to be doing worse than previously and she couldn't stand to witness his silent suffering and not be able to do something about it.

But apart from research, what could she do? It wasn't like she could help unbind the spell. Even if they found it, she would have to be a truly powerful witch to be able to unbind a curse that had lasted for centuries and she was far, far, far from that. She might be the most talented archivist and translator the Coven had known in over a century, but in truth, she was only a burden. If her grandmama hadn't spent so much time trying to discover why Jules was allergic to magic, then maybe she would have been able to discover how to help Bastien.

She sighed. Gods, she wished she could be the one to help him like he had always helped her. He was the only one who could make her feel better about everything from the moment her parents died in the car accident. The only one who could hold her when things got too much.

Of course, there was a limit to even that because he had to leave her when his transformation drew near or hurt her with the magic of it. Without him, she felt lost and alone.

She'd hoped to change that with someone like Simon who might be able to be there for her in ways Violetta and Bastien couldn't. And whom she could be there for in ways she couldn't for her grandmama and best friend.

But hoping and having were two very different things, as she'd been violently reminded last night. It seemed that love, like her magic, was something that remained out of her grasp.

She blinked rapidly, chewing on her lip. She wouldn't cry. Crying never made her feel better. Only work did that. Her work in the library and the charity work she loved to do. Although the latter wasn't filling her time right now as much as it had prior to and just after Christmas. She was in one of those natural lulls between charity drives and the elderly neighbours she visited every week were all away visiting family in other states. So there was very little on her charity works side of things to keep her busy.

So she had planned to completely throw herself into her work in the library over the next few weeks leading up to one of the loneliest times of the year for her. Valentines Day always managed to remind her that she would probably always be alone.

Getting lost in a translation or cataloguing job seemed like a fabulous thing to do right now. Losing track of everything else while she got lost in someone else's words always made the blues fly right away.

"To do that, you need to turn on the lights. Please."

"Right."

Grimacing, she patted her hair to make certain it was still in its neat bun, then ran hands over her favourite flower-print shirt with the capped sleeves to tuck it back into her jeans – damn. Was that a tear? No, just a loose button. Phew. She did it up, then backed carefully away from the mess of boxes she'd fallen over and felt her way along the wall.

The light switch was here somewhere.

There.

Light sprang to life from the wall sconces and chandeliers that were made from old twisting driftwood. Their bulbs lit up the arches of stone and wood with a cheery golden glow. She smiled, breathing in the smell of books – dust and leather and something else that made her yearn to learn everything she could from the words inside.

But before she could get on with her translation work, she needed to deal with the stack of boxes she'd tripped over.

She righted the fallen boxes, noting one of them was open. Half the books were missing from the box. "Damn it."

Why couldn't the interns do what they were told? They knew not to unpack the boxes. Violetta had to do it so she could check the new acquisitions for dark magic – only she could deal with those, logging them and restraining them in the Dark Magics and Dangerous Books Room – and then place the rest in two piles, the ones with magic in them and the ones without. Then Jules, the interns helping with the magical books, had to sort them into piles – what needed to be translated, what could be catalogued and shelved, and what needed to be handled with kid gloves – literally.

But the interns had obviously already got stuck in without Violetta being there, because if Violetta had started unpacking the boxes, she would have moved them to the sorting tables.

Damn it! Where could they have put the items they'd pulled from this box?

The kettle chose that moment to whistle. She turned to the kitchenette.

Stopped.

Bastien stood on the table sniffing at a stack of old books that had been piled there.

Bloody interns. "I don't care if Trevor and Marie are distant family, I'm going to kill them."

FIVE

"Who are you killing this time, dear?" Violetta asked, sticking her head out from the end of the stacks nearest the kitchen.

"Trevor and Marie," she grumbled, gesturing at the books that should never have been put on a surface people ate and drank at. "I assume you didn't put those books there."

"No I did not." She frowned at the books and then glanced towards the kitchen bench. "Before you go about finding them and killing them, do you mind turning that kettle off and making a cup of tea?"

"Fine."

"I'll be right out. I just need to find one more thing." Violetta disappeared back into the stacks again.

Jules picked up Bastien, gave him a quick cuddle then made a pot, letting it steep as she got out Violetta's favourite bone-China teacup and a mug for herself. She quickly poured herself a tea, added two sugars and a good dollop of milk before her grandmama could see and give her the 'tea lecture'.

Turning back to the table, she eyed the books on the edge of it warily. Inched closer. She didn't feel any magic coming from them.

"That doesn't mean anything. Be careful."

Her internal voice was right. Some magic was tricky, especially dark magic.

"You shouldn't stand so close to those books," Violetta said as she came out of the stacks. Her immaculate grey bob swung beside her still-lovely heart-shaped face, her dark brows furrowed as she joined Jules at the table. "Even though Tomaso said there were no magical texts, you know I like to check. I don't want you being hurt like last time."

"I wouldn't need to stand so close to them if Trevor or Marie hadn't unpacked them. They must have done it last night before they left."

"It can't have been them," Violetta said, pouring herself a cup of tea. "The shipment didn't arrive until well after we'd all finished for the day." She tipped her head in that considering way of hers and moved closer to the stack of books and manuscripts, her long violet skirt swaying gently around her legs, the pearls and crystals around her neck making a little clacking sound as she walked.

"Your mother moved like that. Like a dancer."

"Did she? I can't remember that."

"Did you say something, dear?"

"Nope." She sipped her tea as her grandmama gave her the gimlet stare that made people tremble in their boots.

She looked down at her feet.

"You're wearing sneakers, not boots, so you're obviously safe."

"Thanks." She looked back up at her grandmama.

Violetta, eyebrow raised in a perfect arch, returned her attention to the books. "Who could have put these here? I didn't do it, did I, Bastien?" He shook his head. "I didn't think so, but it's good to be sure. You know how distracted I can get when doing my research. I wouldn't put it past myself to start unpacking the boxes without realising it." She tapped her chin in thought then said, "Why are you rubbing your hip like that?"

She stopped rubbing as Violetta frowned at her. "I didn't see the boxes and fell over one."

"Then why did you say you were fine? Honestly, Julianna, it doesn't do anyone any good when you lie about getting hurt. Do I need to call Doctor Pilar?"

"No! I'm fine." The last thing she needed was Doctor Pilar coming over and seeing the cuts and scratches all over her torso. He'd tell Violetta and then she'd get The Lecture. Although, she would definitely get The Lecture when she told Violetta about what had happened with Simon. Despite knowing last night she needed her grandmama to fix things for her, she wished she didn't have to tell her about the embarrassing event – it was bad enough Bastien knew – but if she didn't want it getting around that she had no magic ...

"It's lucky your grandmama is excellent at forgetting spells. Hopefully she'll wind a little something extra into Simon's that will make him cower every time he so much as sees tomato or basil again."

"I don't want her to punish him."

"It's no less than he deserves."

"You don't mean that."

"Of course I do."

An image of Simon cowering before a stand of tomatoes at the supermarket spun into her mind, but no matter how gratifying it would be to see it, she couldn't allow it. What had happened wasn't truly his fault. It was hers. She'd been too desperate to find love. She had to face facts – it just wasn't going to happen for her. She had her grandmama, Bastien, and her work. That would have to be enough.

She met Violetta's gaze and told her what had happened.

"Julianna! You should have told me the instant it happened. Not only should Dr Pilar have been called last night, who knows how many people Simon has told by now!"

"Well, you were out. And I doubt he's told anyone apart from his mother. The clean-up was extensive. Besides, I think he was hoping to blackmail you with the knowledge, so that wouldn't work if he told people."

"Julianna, that's not the point."

"It's exactly the point."

Violetta glared at her. "Well, I'm calling Dr Pilar just to check you out."

"Please don't. Bastien helped fix me up last night—"

"Bastien knew!" she said, glaring at the black cat winding around Jules' feet.

"I said I'd tell you this morning. And I have. You can now go and wipe Simon's memory – his mother's too if needed – but please don't do anything else. It was my stupidity that caused the problem. So please promise you won't do more than wipe the event from his memory." She stared down her grandmama's gimlet glare.

"Very well," Violetta said after a long, tense moment. "I will figure out the best spell and take care of it this afternoon."

"Thank you."

Violetta reached a comforting hand out but pulled back before she could make contact. "Are you certain you're okay?"

"Yes. Please don't worry." She tried a smile, but it came out a bit wobbly, so she turned her attention to the books on the table. "All I want to do is get stuck into these. They look fascinating." She took a step closer to the end of the table the books were stacked on, tripped over the edge of a rug and lost her grip on her tea mug. It soared out of her hand, the tea flying out of the mug right towards the stack of old manuscripts, journals and grimoires. "No!" she cried as she hit the edge of the table.

"Watch out!"

Jules knew the cry wasn't for the books. She threw herself sideways, landing hard on the floor on the other side of the table as Violetta thrust her hands out, a small amount of power sparking around her. Jules pushed up and crawled around the kitchen island, trying to get further away from the magic that, even though minimal, was a thousand needles pricking her skin. Her stomach heaved.

She grasped for the bin just in time, vomiting up all her breakfast.

"Julianna, I'm so sorry. Are you okay?" Violetta stood above her, hands half stretched towards her.

"Yes. Yes. Don't worry about me. See, not even bleeding." She held out her arms. "I'm fine." She wiped her mouth. "What about the books?"

Violetta's mouth worked for a moment before she gave a little nod – thank the Goddess she wasn't about to carry on apologising about using magic around Jules. "I saved them." Violetta pointed across the room.

Jules pulled herself up and leaned, trembling, against the centre bench. Tea was splattered across the table, dripping off the edges, but thankfully the pile of old and fragile grimoires, journals and books had been transported across the room and sat in two piles on Jules' desk in the far corner of the room. "Thank the Goddess. I thought I'd ruined them. You see, that's why you never put books on the kitchen table! Especially with klutzes like me around."

"Are you sure you're okay, dear?"

"Your transportation spell was minimal, so I'm fine. Stop fussing." She waved her hand and moved out from behind the centre bench, almost tripping over the rug just beyond it. Before Violetta could say anything, she said, "I just need to clean up here and then get back to work. I gather since you put those on my desk, there's no magic in them."

"I don't feel anything – which matches with Tomaso's assurances. You'll be safe from them at least."

"Grandmama."

Violetta's nostrils flared as she turned away and gestured to the boxes at the base of the stairs. "I didn't realise Tomaso was sending so many," she said airily. "They'll keep you busy for a while.

"I can't wait," she said, meaning it more than she'd ever meant it before. She needed to be distracted from the disaster that was her love life. And about the looming lone-liness of another Valentine's Day spent without a lover. Pushing the depressing thought aside, she began to clean up the mess she'd made.

As Violetta began to help her clean up, she was mindful that the older witch watched her every movement. It took a bit of effort, but Jules hid the twinges of pain pinging all over her body – she really didn't want her grandmama to feel guilty over hurting her. Finally, with a suppressed sigh, she gave the table a final wipe, rinsed the cloth then headed to her desk.

"Well, I'll leave you to it then. I've got a few things I

want to finish here before I go and deal with Simon and his mother."

Her tone was so ominous, Jules felt compelled to say, "Grandmama, you promised."

Violetta sighed. "I know." She picked up her tea and walked back towards the stacks, her purple skirt swishing around her knees, crystals and beads clicking and clacking in an almost hypnotic rhythm as she went.

Bastien jumped up onto the desk and rubbed against Jules, meowing at her. Giving him a long stroke from head to tail, she turned to the books on her desk. "So, Grandmama is doing her work, how about I get stuck into mine?" Bastien meowed at her in response. She really wished she could mind-speak with him like other witches could with their Familiars – but she was not a normal witch, nor was he a normal Familiar – but it seemed to be an enthusiastic meow. "Which one should I start with?"

He patted the oldest-looking journal on top of the pile to the left. "Good pick." It was the one she was most drawn to – its age calling to her along with the ancient Roman letters scrawled on the front.

"My Life of Magic in the Service of Vesta by Esta Stevius of the Vestal Virgin Coven," she translated.

Vestal Virgins! Oh Goddess!

A frisson of excitement chased over her skin. Shivering a little, she pulled on her cotton gloves before taking the journal to place it gently on the cradle in front of her.

"Now, what secrets do you have to tell me?" she whispered as she opened the leather-bound parchment.

Bastien, rather than sit in her lap as he usually did, perched on the desk, his gaze on the journal as if he meant to read along with her. She stroked her hand over his back as she started to read, but after a few pages, forgot all about him, lost in the unfolding story before her.

Images formed in her mind as she read, so real it was almost like she'd been there and seen it herself.

"You have."

"What?" Her heart thumped hard and fast in her chest.

"Read on."

"Okay."

Jules turned the page carefully, the cotton gloves startlingly white against the yellowing pages of parchment.

Her breathing came in little gasps as her eyes scanned the words, her brain doing an automatic translation.

Her nightmares. Her dreams. They were all here. On the pages of this ancient journal. How could that be?

She turned another page, her lips moving now as she whispered the words before she'd even translated them in her mind. She knew. She knew this. She'd witnessed in her nightmares repeatedly the horror as Lianna Stevius, Vesta's chosen vessel for the powers she wished to give to humanity, was torn from her lover, from her child, cursed and buried alive.

She didn't need to read the words to know that was what had happened – she'd woken screaming from the horror nearly every night of her life, the memory of dirt raining down, choking her, darkness smothering her, gasping for breath until ... until there were no more breaths. Though she'd never truly remembered those dreams in the detail written here, just the way they made her feel, she remembered them all now.

And even though she knew where the story led, she couldn't stop herself from reading the words Esta Stevius had written 2,000 years ago about the punishment that turned the servant into a cat who'd been so kind to her and Lianna.

His name had been Bastieno.

Bastien.

Oh Goddess. Was this why he was cursed? Because he'd helped a Vestal Virgin be with her lover?

A Vestal Virgin whose memories had played in her dreams and nightmares all her life.

That could only mean ... "No," she breathed, unable to believe it.

"Believe it. It's true."

"Lianna?"

"Yes."

She winced as pain spiked through her eye. But she couldn't stop herself from reading because she couldn't believe what was in front of her eyes.

The curse. Esta had written it down. She read it, lips moving over the words. Her skin prickled and hairs rose all over her body, but she couldn't seem to stop.

Bastien howled and struck out at her hand as she went to turn the page, then leaped at her as she rocked back in shock, his movement enough to make her chair roll back from her desk to smack into the wall a metre behind her.

"Julianna!" Her grandmama's voice, a panicked cry, rang out from deep in the stacks. The sound of running echoed hollowly, coming closer until Violetta burst out of the end of the stacks in the middle of the room, eyes wide, face filled with fear as she raced over to Jules. "Julianna. I felt magic. You're bleeding."

Jules looked down at her hand where a line of blood welled across the back of her hand. "Bastien swiped at me. He stopped me from reading the curse in that journal." She gestured at it, her mind swirling with images from her nightmares and dreams.

"Memories. Not dreams."

Violetta gasped. "Oh, my Goddess. Where did you get this?" She snatched up the journal. "Did you read this?"

Jules nodded slowly, still so shocked that she wasn't bothered by the fact Violetta had picked up the ancient journal without gloves on. "I don't understand. It's the dream. The nightmare. The one that's tormented me ever since I can remember. It's written in there. How can that be?"

Violetta's large name-sake eyes slowly rose to focus on her. "I was right. You *are* cursed, my dear."

"What? How does she know that?"

Violetta's words – and those of her internal voice – snapped her out of her stupor. "Don't be ridiculous. How can I be cursed? Who would bother to curse me?"

Violetta tapped the journal. "It's in here. I've only ever remembered the latter parts of my life as Esta – my most recent reincarnations are far clearer – but now, seeing this, I remember more. I know who you are."

Bastien made a sound of surprise, his head snapping up to stare at Violetta as if seeing her for the first time.

"He recognises her."

"Oh Goddess. Oh Goddess. It's true."

"I knew your soul was old. I just didn't realise how old. But this explains so much. I always wondered why you couldn't remember at least part of who you'd been – it's highly unusual for a reincarnated witch or warlock not to remember at least some of their past lives."

"No." Jules pushed up from the desk, took a step back. "I'm not an old soul. I don't carry that kind of power."

"Yes. You do. And you are. You were Lianna Stevius. And Bastien was ..."

"The servant who helped the demi-god and Lianna be together."

Violetta frowned at her for a moment but then said, "Yes. I remember now. It's why he's always been bound to our family like he has. Why his curse has lasted this long. But now you've found this, now you remember – we can free you both."

"How?"

"Go to Rome. Unbind the curse."

"What? How? I can't go to Rome."

"But you must." She tapped the journal. "You know how curses work. We don't have the original witch who cast it. But we do have the words and three souls who were there – and now you remember, we can find where it was cast and undo the evil that was done so long ago."

"But don't we have to do it on an anniversary?"

"Yes."

"But when is that?"

"It's all in here. You just read it."

"Not that bit!"

Violetta flipped open the journal and pointed at the date written on the page at the start of the section Jules had just read. "If I know my ancient Roman calendars right – and I do – the anniversary is on the thirteenth of February."

"Valentine's Day Eve? But today's the second. That means we've not even got two weeks!"

"Then you better hurry up and pack. I'll book your flights to Rome. Bastien and I will go via portal and meet you there. Come on, hurry up. We don't have time to waste."

Jules stared at her grandmama for a moment, all the

excuses why it was impossible swirling in her mind. She opened her mouth, about to voice them when her internal voice – the original Julianna who had apparently been talking to her all these years – said, *"It's our last chance, Jules. It's Bas' last chance."*

She snapped her mouth shut, jumped up and ran towards the stairs. It might seem totally insane but she had only just been wailing to herself about her inability to do something to help Bas. But now here was something she could do, and despite her doubts, she was going to do it.

CHAPTER
SIX

J   ules thrust the shutters open and looked out at the
    plaza below, busy with people returning from a day of
    work or sightseeing, and now looking for a place to
eat dinner.

She couldn't believe she'd slept the day away due to
jetlag – why hadn't anyone woken her? They had so few
days as it was with her having to figure this all out by
midnight on Valentine's Eve – talk about cutting it close!
Why couldn't she have found the journal a year ago?

Although, Violetta hadn't seemed terribly worried
about losing another day when she'd checked on her an
hour ago. She'd said they couldn't find the exact place the
curse was cast down in the Forum until after all the tourists
were back in their hotels and *pensiones* for the night. Apparently the only thing Bastien could remember about that
night was that the curse was placed in the Vestal Virgin's
garden. While the temple was merely a ruin and their
gardens mostly nothing but dirt, they at least knew roughly
where to start their search.

It was a large area though and they needed all the time

they could get as far as Jules was concerned. And because her jetlag had been so bad, they'd lost an entire day.

Her grandmama might not be worried, but she was. It was now the fifth, which meant she only had a week to find where the curse was cast and figure out the bits that were missing from Esta's journal so that they'd be successful on the night. The young Vestal witch had been so traumatised that there were parts of what Clodia had done that she didn't remember, like how the High Priestess had managed to bind and hold a demi-God and a witch with the powers of a Goddess.

Jules was certain those were some important bits of information they'd need to discover if they wanted to break the curse. Not to mention what had happened to the demi-God who was supposed to be her soulmate and forever love and where they could find him.

Pain stabbed her through the eye and she clutched her head.

"You can't think about him."

"Really?" It still blew her mind to think the voice she'd heard all her life was an ancient part of her reincarnated soul. *"Anything else you want to tell me?"*

"I'm trying. But the curse doesn't allow me to tell you much."

"Well, if you can't help me, how am I meant to discover any of what I need to know?"

Silence greeted her question.

"This is going to be such a disaster," she said out loud.

The shouts of the vendors in the marketplace a few streets away lifted to her. The musical Italian echoed off the cobblestones and ancient brick walls, mingling with the honking horns and the distant roar of cars, trucks, buses and whizzing mopeds. Normally, it would have called to her, making her smile at the incongruity of the ancient mixed with the new, but she was too worried to be charmed.

Although, maybe a walk and a little explore before she was needed tonight would be a good way to work through her thoughts – and work out the kinks she'd gained from the horror that had been the almost 50-hour flight here.

Multiple delays and four stopovers – really, she'd have to make certain she booked the home-leg. Violetta had booked her flights while Jules read the journal, grappling with the fact she was the reincarnation of Lianna Stevius and was cursed.

Of course, her grandmama had no idea about booking plane travel given she always used her magic to transport herself places – like she'd transported herself and Bastien here after dropping Jules at the airport. Another reason to hate her non-magical status. Something that would hopefully be fixed once she had vanquished the curse. Perhaps wandering around the ancient city might jog some memories or enable the voice to tell her more.

Thankfully, she was free to do so. Her grandmama's friend, Tomaso, had smoothed things here with the Roman Coven and there were no restrictions to where they could go or what they could do. He'd also organised accommodation at this lovely villa. It was run as a pensione by an elderly couple, but he'd paid for the entire place to ensure their privacy and sent the elderly couple on a holiday to visit their daughter who now lived in America.

She'd found all of this out from Violetta when she'd arrived. Her grandmama had called her old friend to tell him about what they had discovered immediately upon sending Jules off to pack and he had jumped at the challenge. Jules had been surprised to hear Violetta had shared so much with him, but then again, he was one of her grand-parents' oldest friends. Apparently, she'd met him when she was little, but she couldn't remember.

She was looking forward to meeting him now, though, but he had been off talking to contacts, trying to get some older maps of the Forum to help them find the exact spot the curse was cast. And now, according to Violetta, he was at the Forum scoping out where the security guards were, as well as trying a few different cloaking spells they could use that wouldn't affect Jules. They really couldn't let anyone see what they were doing down there.

Violetta had gone down to the Forum by herself every night since arriving here to jog memories of her life as Esta.

Maybe she should do the same.

"You already know what you need to know."

"Do I?"

"You know the players and the words of the curse. Work backwards from there. Remember all you've seen."

"My nightmares and dreams? You know I can't access them properly."

"Try."

She closed her eyes and tried to think back to the horror of images she'd woken from a few hours ago, but they remained as elusive as always. *"I can't do it. Why do you expect me to do what Bastien and Violetta are failing to do?"* Bastien couldn't talk about that night – every time he tried, he suffered horrible pain that caused his nose to bleed, and bruises to bloom all over his body. And Violetta also seemed blocked from a great deal of Esta's memories.

"At least she's trying."

"That's not fair. I'm trying too."

"Not enough. Don't you want to free yourself? Free Bastien?"

"You know I do." She would do anything for him.

He had to be freed of the curse. Nobody but the ancient Gods would think he deserved to go on being punished for helping Lianna be with her lover. He deserved everything good. He certainly deserved more than to be locked to her friendship and service. He deserved to be lo—

Pain spiked behind her eye and she let out a hiss, closing her eye and pressing her finger against the orb.

The door opened behind her and she turned, hand still to her eye. "Bastien," she said, a smile widening on her face. He'd just showered after his change, his short black hair still a bit damp with comb marks in it. He'd dressed in a favourite soft blue t-shirt – had it always highlighted the breadth of his shoulders, the muscles in his arms and chest like that? – and a worn pair of jeans that sat low on his hips and looked a little looser than they had when she'd seen him wearing them before she'd left to catch her flight.

Had he not been eating enough? His change always used up so much energy. She'd have to make certain he took better care of himself now she was here. "I was wondering where you were. I expected you to come back right after you changed."

"Sorry, I was held up." A strange expression crossed his face. Come to think of it, he looked a little grey.

"Are you okay?"

"Absolutely. I'm a little hungry though. Do you want to come down to the kitchen while I get something to eat?"

"Sure." She moved away from the window. "Is Grandmama or Tomaso back yet? I want to ask them if they've found any more information about Lianna's lov— Ow!" She grabbed her head, staggered, then sat with a plop on the bed.

"You really need to get a hang of these curse-rules."

57

"You think?"

"Jules!" Bastien raced across the room to her. "Are you okay?"

She dropped her hand and forced a smile. "I'm fine. See. I obviously can't think about either of us deserving lo—" It hit her so hard this time she was flung backwards, the bed thankfully making a soft landing. "Ow. Damn it to hell and back."

"How are we supposed to do this if we can't even think about what we can't think about?"

"Don't ask me. I've never been able to figure it out. Ow. That hurts!"

SEVEN

Bastien sat on the bed beside Jules, not quite knowing what to do. She hated anyone fussing over her but Gods, how he hated seeing her in such distress. He touched her arm. "Jules?" When that didn't get a response, he tangled his fingers in hers, pulling her hand away from her face then stroked her forehead until the tension he could feel there softened.

She let out a little sigh, tilting her head into his caress. "What would I do without you, Bastien?"

He wished he could tell her that she'd never have to find out.

She sat up slowly and sighed. "You've endured this for almost 2,000 years. How have you stayed sane? I've only known about my curse for three days and I feel like I'm going to lose my shit any second."

"You're stronger than you think."

She sighed, the sound full of unsaid things that made him wish once again that he could drag Clodia to Tartarus and hand her over to his great uncle to receive the reward she so richly deserved for doing this to them. He wanted to tell Jules how special she was. That he was certain she would be the one to discover how to break the curse. It wasn't just that she shared her full name – Julianna – with his Lianna – all the reincarnations were named Julianna, a strange twist of the curse. It was everything else, including the fact she had preferred to be called Jules, stamping her difference from the moment she could talk.

Keenly intelligent with a thirst for knowledge that shaped everything she did, she was far lonelier than any version who'd come before because she seemed to be far more aware of all that was missing in her life. It was like she could feel the power trapped deep inside her – given Clodia didn't get the powers that night, they had to have returned to Lianna at some stage, the curse making it so they were locked away from her. He should have realised that long ago, but it was Violetta who voiced the thought after they arrived here. They couldn't truly know though until the curse was broken. And if things went wrong, she might lose the chance to have access to her powers forever.

Violetta had told Jules about the possibility she'd get her magic back once the curse was gone as soon as she'd arrived – and he'd never seen her so happy. She'd spent her life trying to figure out why she, of all their family, didn't have any magic, often blaming herself or thinking herself somehow wrong, or weak.

But she wasn't weak. Far from it. If she was, she would never have asked her parents and Violetta from the age of four why she couldn't use her power. And when they had no true answers for her, she'd researched and researched and researched and researched. To no avail, of course. Nothing was written about the curse she was under, and the curse itself made it difficult for her to think of other things that might tip her off as to what the issue was.

But even the fact she questioned had shown how extraordinary she was and had given him hope through all these years. None of the other incarnations had seemed curious about why they were non-magical at all.

Then there were her dreams and nightmares. She could never talk about them, but he knew they were memories from things she said while in the grip of them. None of the others had ever had any kind of access to their past lives' memories.

Also, she looked eerily like Lianna in a way none of the others ever had, right down to the heart-shaped face, the auburn hair with the white streak and the green flecks in her topaz eyes.

And there was the fact that none of the other incarnations had ever responded to him like she did. He'd only ever been a guard or sentinel with the others. But with Jules, from her earliest years, he was a companion, teaching, guarding, listening. Then, as she'd moved into adulthood, he'd become her friend. Her best friend.

Her only friend.

But for him, she was so much more than just a friend.

He loved her so much. So deeply. More deeply than he'd ever thought he could. It was a living hell not to be able to tell her.

Jules sighed again, the sound full of a deep sadness that made his heart ache.

He would be happy to ride out this torment if only he could comfort her properly. If only he could make her sadness fade away and fill the space with happiness, fulfilment and the love she deserved. The love she'd had within her grasp and would still have but for the wickedness of a witch who'd grasped for power that wasn't hers and had lashed out with a curse in an act of possessive revenge.

Jules knew of the curse now, knew of Lianna's demi-God lover – but until the curse was broken, she would never see that he was the lover and that he treasured her more than he'd treasured anything in his long life. That she had never been, and would never be, alone.

He squeezed her hand in the absence of the words he longed to say, the words she longed to hear. She sniffed and moved her hand to rub at her face.

She was crying?

"Jules? Why are you crying? You know you can do this, don't you? I believe in you. We all do."

She sniffed again, then leaned against him, her head on his shoulder. "I know. It's not that so much as …" She took in a deep, shuddering breath. "This is going to sound so selfish and horrible, but I just realised that if I do succeed, you won't be with me like this anymore. What am I going to do without you?"

What? He pulled back to look at her aura – it was a bit muddy and thin, as if she was pulling it into herself in protection. What was going on in that intricate mind of hers? "What are you talking about?"

She stroked her finger down the side of his face. "You were bound to my family – to me—" She coughed. "Because of the curse. But once it's gone, you'll be free. You can go and live your life however you choose."

She turned and cupped his face. "And I want you to go. I want you to be free to live the life that was taken from you all those years ago. To have everything you lost. And I promise, I will make sure you have everything you need to do whatever you want to do. You deserve far more out of life than to be tied to me and my family for a moment longer. It's just, I'm going to miss not having you as a friend anymore. Not like this anyway."

What the ever-loving-fuck? She thought he'd leave her? But before he could disabuse her of that notion, she barrelled on.

"I'm sure it will be a relief not to be tied to me anymore. And you don't need to worry about me – if you are – because if my magic is freed as you all think it will be, then I'll need to learn how to use it. Bit pathetic to go back to school at almost 30, but beggars can't be choosers, right? At least, on the bright side, I'll be able to start to date within the magical community. Maybe fall in love and have that love returned." She winced. "That'd be nice, right?"

What? She wanted to fall in love with someone else? Had she forgotten about her demi-God lover – him – and that they'd finally have a chance to be together?

But of course, that was just his wishful thinking. Despite the fact Jules was so like Lianna in looks and, in some degree, temperament, she was very different from her in other ways.

She was a modern woman in a modern world. She wanted love, but she also wanted many other things – Lianna had been perfectly happy to think only of their life together, the children they would have, the home and family they would build. Jules had her charities and her work and both were very important to her. And with her magical powers in her control, she'd naturally want to explore what she could do to help others better and what more she could do within her career path without being encumbered by someone her soul had loved in some distant past.

He'd always thought she would just want what Lianna wanted. But that wasn't true.

She might not choose him at all.

The thought sliced through him, hard enough, painful enough to make him jerk back.

"Bastien? Are you okay?" She steadied him. "I knew you lied to me last night when I arrived. The changes are getting worse, aren't they? It's why you took so long after your change to come in here, isn't it?"

"It's fine. I—"

A knock at the door pulled him from his depressing thoughts.

Power sang to him from the other side of the door.

Tamuel.

"That must be Grandmama." Jules jumped up from the bed before he could stop her.

"Jules, wait!"

Too late though, she was already at the door, opening it.

"I'm ready, Grandmama—" The words died on her lips as the door swung wide showing who stood in the hallway. She stumbled back a few steps. "Who are you?" she asked, her voice tight, pained.

"Tamuel! Mind your power," Bastien said through their cupid mind-speak.

The cupid, in his older gentleman persona, bowed, his aura pulsing then pulling back towards him. "I'm sorry. They told me you were sensitive but I didn't realise how much. Forgive me?"

EIGHT

The suave elderly gentleman sauntered into the room, causing Jules to stumble away from him.

She backed up until she hit the wall. How had she not noticed the difference in power radiating through the door? Violetta was powerful, but nothing like this. And even though this man had pulled it back, her skin still prickled so much she had to put some distance between them.

"Who is he?"

"I don't know."

"He feels ..."

"Familiar."

"Yes."

She watched him warily as he crossed to shake Bastien's hand. "You're looking a bit grey, my friend."

"You know each other?"

"We're old friends. Aren't we, Bas?" His accent lilted like the Italian ones lifting from the plaza below her window, but with a slight difference in cadence. She struggled to look away from him, especially when he caught her gaze with his twinkling black eyes. Her skin prickled with the danger evident in him. Someone with that much power would always be dangerous to her, no matter their intentions for good.

"Touch him."

"Are you crazy? He's too powerful."

"He won't hurt you."

"Tomaso di Erosi, at your service," he said, extending his hand.

"Don't touch him," Bastien snapped, moving between them.

"Aw, Bas, don't be like that," he said, pulling his hand back. "I won't hurt her. That's the last thing I want."

"Then you should keep your power to yourself like you've been told."

"True." Tomaso laughed out loud, the sound ringing in the air, twining around Jules, making her want to laugh with him. There was something that felt ... familiar about it. Like the laughter of a friend you hadn't seen for a while.

"May I?" He gestured to the chair at the desk, but before she could even nod, he'd walked over to it. He unbuttoned his immaculate steel-blue suit blazer, exposing the snowy white and expensive-looking shirt underneath, its two top buttons undone to show off the strong column of his tanned neck and a few inches of chest, and sat down. He ran his large hands along his suit pants and looked up at her, black eyes twinkling as if he were overjoyed.

His salt-and-pepper hair was cut short in a way that showed off the strong waves. His eyebrows were thick, black and straight, yet didn't overwhelm the strong patrician lines of his face. There was something oddly familiar about him – maybe because she had met him when a toddler, even though she couldn't remember – something that made her want to draw closer, to touch him.

"Then touch him. Take his hand."

She took a few steps towards him. "Nice to meet you finally. Grandmama has spoken about you a lot over the years."

"As she has you." His smile widened. "She has kept me up to date with your progress since I met you when you were but a babe."

"Really?"

"But of course. Your little problem has been a particular fascination." He rubbed his hands together. "Breaking such a powerful curse – what a feather in my cap that will be."

She frowned at him. "This isn't a game to me."

His smile disappeared, his gaze intent. "I can assure you, it's not a game to me either. I take this very seriously. But to be involved in such an endeavour after so many years of ... boredom. You have to excuse my excitement."

She nodded, even though it seemed a bit weird to be excited about all this. Terrified, worried, angry, frustrated – all good. Excited – not so much.

"So, shall we be friends?" He held his hand out.

"Tomaso!" Bastien snapped again. "Stop it."

Tomaso frowned and then said, "I'm sorry. I know I shouldn't touch her given her magical allergy, but something is telling me otherwise."

"Well ignore it," Bas said, sounding more pissed off than she'd ever heard him sound.

She wouldn't have told him to ignore it. She would have commented that what he'd said was a strange thing to say ... if only she wasn't feeling the same way. Instead of saying any of that though, she said to Bas, "It's fine." He didn't seem like he believed her. "I promise," she said, moving past Bastien to stand in front of the other man. "I can't feel anything from him now." It was strange, given how much power she'd felt only moments ago. And she really did want to touch him because, like he'd said, there was something telling her she should.

"That's me," the voice said.

She shook her head at it. *"No. It's not just you. There's something ... unreal about him. Something that maybe touching him might reveal."*

"Go with that then."

Warily, she grasped Tomaso's outstretched hand.

Her jaw slammed closed and her fingers spasmed around his, tightening. She tried to let go, but she couldn't. She couldn't. Was it the magic he was pushing down deep inside himself in an effort to protect her? Maybe. Probably.

Oh Goddess. She'd made a mistake. She braced for the slashing pain as her body rejected his magic.

It didn't come. Instead, the room swirled around her as images flickered to life in her head. She pitched forward, falling, falling ...

"Jules! Jules!" Bas couldn't see what was going on - damn this blindness that afflicted him in his human form - but he knew something terrible was happening.

Jules' aura had flared out wide and then gone black for a moment before returning to a faded version of her usually jewel-bright self. He could still see it well enough though to see her crash to her knees, taking Tam down with her.

Not that he cared about the cupid. He'd done this to her. "Tam, what did you do? What the fuck did you do?" he said, racing forward, grabbing Jule's hand, trying to remove it from Tamuel's grip. But it wouldn't loosen. Both of them were holding on to the other as if they were stuck with superglue. "Tam, let go. Let go damn you!"

Tamuel didn't answer. Bas glanced over at the cupid. His aura was strange too, especially the bit that was around his head where his eyes were. That part was swirling madly. So madly, Bas had to look away because it was making him feel sick.

At least Jules wasn't reacting like she did to magic - which meant this wasn't a magical problem. That at least gave him a little relief, because if she was being exposed to magic for this long, the way she'd been reacting lately, it might tear her apart.

"Jules. Jules, please," he begged, giving up on trying to separate their hands and moving close to cup her face. "Jules, please come back to me. Come back now."

Nothing. She didn't move, didn't make a sound, just remained there on her knees, body completely rigid, aura so pale and strange, holding on to Tamuel's hand.

Footsteps sounded down the hallway, moving fast, coming closer. He jumped as the door banged open and Violetta's familiar form – her distinctive violet-tinged aura giving her away – rushed into the room. "Bas, what happened?"

"You felt that?" he asked as she came down beside him.

"No. I felt nothing. I heard you shouting as I was coming up the street. What happened?"

"Jules took Tomaso's hand in hers."

"That is all?"

"Yes."

"He was holding his magic in obeisance?"

"Yes. As it is now." Somehow the cupid hadn't let an ounce of his magic seep out of him despite whatever was happening to him. At least Bas, with his minimal magical ability, couldn't feel anything.

"Thank the Goddess."

Apparently, neither could Violetta.

She reached out as if to touch Jules but then pulled her hand back, which he was grateful for given her power wasn't as well contained as Tamuel's was. It was fluctuating in her aura which indicated it pulsed just below her skin. Jules would definitely react to it if Violetta touched her right now.

"Any ideas on how we can separate them?" Bas asked her as she sat there at his side, wringing her hands in an uncharacteristic show of her emotional state.

"No. I think we just have to wait for one of them to let go."

"How long will that be?"

She shrugged - at least, he thought she shrugged given her aura moved up and down around her shoulders. "I am as in the dark as you are. I've never seen anything like this before."

"Neither have I," he said.

"Maybe move behind her, Bas, in case she falls backwards. We don't want her hitting her head and doing herself some damage at this point."

"No." Although, whatever was happening might be causing damage enough. But they would know nothing until one of them came out of whatever this was.

He moved to kneel behind Jules, his hands on her shoulders, supporting her. Violetta moved closer to Tamuel but didn't touch him - the cupid wouldn't be hurt by such a short fall to the floor if one of them let go of the other. Not that Violetta knew he was a cupid, but she wasn't strong enough to hold the bigger man up anyway, so there was little point her doing what Bas was doing for Jules.

They sat there waiting for what seemed like forever before Tamuel suddenly gasped and fell backwards onto the floor, his hand slipping from Jules' grip.

Jules collapsed backwards into his waiting arms, her body as limp as a rag. "Jules," he said, not caring his voice sounded endlessly broken, wishing he could see her properly.

He was vaguely aware of Violetta shouting. He looked up at her and realised she was asking about the woman in his arms. "She's breathing. Unconscious but breathing."

"Thank the Goddess."

"How's Tomaso?" he asked as the cupid groaned and rolled over onto his side.

"Crap. Tomaso!" Violetta said, lunging towards him as if she too had just remembered he was there. "Tomaso, are you okay?" she asked at the same time Bas asked, "What happened?"

"Whoa, whoa. One question at a time," the cupid masquerading as an older man said. He clutched at his head and moaned again. "Hades' balls, that hurts."

Violetta reached towards him, power sparking just under her skin, but then pulled her hands back. "I'm sorry, I can't use any healing powers on you here. Not with Jules in the room."

"That's fine. It's fine. I don't need it." He waved away her help and pushed himself upright, edging back to lean against the wall. "That's not better at all," he mumbled. "How's Jules?"

"Unconscious. Breathing. Aside from that, I don't know," Bas snapped. "What did you do?"

The cupid shrugged and made a wincing sound. "I don't

know. I certainly didn't intend it to happen. I thought I was just shaking her hand."

"So you don't know what you did?" Violetta asked.

"Didn't I just say that?"

"No need to be snarky."

"Sorry. But my head is hurting like a *bastardo* and my brain feels as mushy as uncooked *panna cotta*."

"And you have no idea why?"

"No. Nothing like that has ever happened before."

"Well that's concerning."

"Yes. It is. Particularly as I can't remember anything from after I took her hand in mine until just now."

"You can't remember anything?"

"No." He frowned. "Well, there was something. A flash of images, but I can't make sense of them right now. Maybe after I've had time to decompress and get rid of this Gods-awful headache, then I'll be able to make more sense of it. But until that time, maybe it would be best to get Jules onto the bed where she can rest properly and then we can all go downstairs and figure out what to do next."

"I'm not leaving her," Bas said. "Not until she wakes up."

"What if she doesn't."

"What if she doesn't what?"

"Wake up?"

Bas shook his head wildly as Violetta said, "No. Not an option. She will wake up. She has to."

"Yes," Bas said firmly. "You woke up. She will too. We just need to give her time to come out of whatever this is." He looked down at his love lying so quietly in his arms. "Buy you are right, I should move her to the bed. You go downstairs with Violetta where she can help you with your headache. Then when you're ready, come back up here and we'll discuss what to do next in this room."

"I don't think—" Tamuel began.

"You don't get a say," Violetta said, making a chopping motion. "Bas is in charge of things while she is like this. So let's allow him to get Jules settled and we'll go take care of your aching head." She stood and said to Bas, "We'll be back as soon as I've taken care of Tomaso. Look after our girl."

"I will."

Violetta helped a groaning Tamuel to his feet and then they left the room. Bas picked Jules up and carried her over to the bed, placing her down as gently as he could. He covered her legs with the soft blanket and then sat on the bed beside her, pulling her into his arms again, holding her close.

And as he sat there waiting for her to wake or Tam and Violetta to come back, he prayed to all the Gods in all the heavens that Jules would be okay.

She had to be okay. He couldn't live a moment longer if something happened to her. Her end would be his end this time. He wouldn't live without Jules. He couldn't.

CHAPTER
NINE

J ules fell in the darkness but then suddenly, the falling sensation disappeared as quickly as it had come.

She opened her eyes with a start to look up into a face that was bewilderingly familiar.

It was her face, she realised with a start. Although there were slight differences in the nose and skin colour, the arch of the brow.

Wetness landed on her face. Was it raining? One of the drops rolled across her cheek and into her mouth – salty.

Not rain, tears. The woman who looked like her, who held her, was crying. Why was she crying?

The image flipped and suddenly she was no longer looking up at the woman but *was* the woman looking down at the baby in her arms. A baby still covered in the mess of a fresh birthing.

"My baby boy."

She lifted a trembling hand, stroking down the side of the baby's face, her vision starring. Pain, grief and an overwhelming love stole her breath as she stared at the new-born in her arms. "Please. Don't blame him for my transgressions. He's an innocent," she whispered.

The baby gurgled and she bent to kiss his beautiful forehead, to breathe in the scent of him, but Clodia was already there, reaching to take him.

Lianna tried to hold on, to keep him with her for a moment longer, but the High Priestess turned away, pushing the baby into little Esta's arms. "We will need his power. Put him in place in the pentacle." Esta hesitated. "Do it now, girl, or I will use all your power and I will not be gentle about it."

"No!" Lianna cried, trying to move, to reach out to her new-born son. The golden bands on her arms tightened and weakness overwhelmed her so she could barely breathe.

Across the pentacle, another voice cried out. "Don't do this, Clodia. My aunt can't possibly want this."

Sebastio. He was here? How had Clodia bound him? This wasn't possible – was it? She scrabbled onto all fours, trying to peer through the night, but she couldn't see him, could only hear him as he continued to yell at Clodia, voice ringing with panic and rage as he fought against whatever held him here.

Clodia did not have the power to bind a demi-God for a few minutes, let alone the power it had taken to make her pregnancy to come to fruition in half the time, her demi-God-warlock son growing inside her even faster than any of them had thought possible. It must be that blood-red gem Clodia had been wearing since the night the High Priestess had captured them.

The bands on her arms tightened again, taking more power, more energy. She screamed.

"Lianna!" Sebastio called out. "Stop it, Clodia. You're hurting her."

"Do you think I care?" the High Priestess shrieked. "She broke the law. Committed treason. For this, she deserves to lose all her power and more."

"Because of you. You gave her no choice."

"She always had a choice, and she chose to lay with you over her vows, over her obligations to Vesta and to *Roma*."

"Because of you. Because of your greed. Your lust for power. You set this in motion. You planned for us to meet knowing we were matched by the Fates."

"Clever of you to have figured that out. But it will change nothing now."

"You cannot do this. The powers belong to her, not you. The Gods will not allow such hubris."

"My hubris? What about yours? And if they were so concerned, surely your father would be here now to stop me."

Sounds of struggling. "I will make you pay."

"You and your army of cats."

Lianna gasped. What did she mean? Sebastio was a cupid, a son of Eros, a cupid of the Greek and Roman Pantheons, not Bastet with her army of cats in the Egyptian Pantheon.

Clodia's cackle filled the air as she lifted her arms and began to incant her spell. Lianna cried out as more power was pulled from her, twisted and warped to obey Clodia's will and not her own. Across the pentacle, her servant, Bastieno, cried out in pain and disappeared from her sight. No. No.

Sebastio yelled, still trying to stop the mad High Priestess, but there was no point. She'd wanted this all along. Sebastio was right, Clodia had set this into motion. And then she'd made certain Lianna was found guilty of treason after she found Lianna with her lover.

The priests of *Roma* and her fellow Vestal priestesses had helped Clodia further bind Lianna's powers and kept her imprisoned until the birth of her baby. Of course, they thought she had months to go until that time, but Clodia had other plans. She needed this all to come to fruition before Lianna's service in the Vestal Virgins was over – she'd admitted as much when she'd hidden Lianna away from everyone to hide the speed of the pregnancy. Now Lianna realised she'd sped things along not only so she could steal Lianna's Goddess-given powers while she still had access to them through the arm manacles, but so she could use the birth energy to further her schemes.

"Please, don't use my babe. Not like this."

"I will use him however I wish. He is here, after all, because of my plans; my needs. And he is far more powerful than I ever dreamed. That power will make all the difference."

Oh Gods. She thought the High Priestess was going to bind the baby's magic to her like she had Lianna's, but this was even worse. An act of pure evil.

Clodia was going to use the baby's power to help steal Lianna's Vesta-given powers. She might kill him in the draining of those powers, and there was nothing Lianna could do to stop her. She would be dead soon. Clodia didn't even have to kill her. By *Roma's* laws, for her treason of breaking her vows, she would be shoved into an underground cell, big enough to be considered 'accommodation', with enough food and water to last for a few days. The entrance to the cell would be sealed and filled with dirt. She would suffocate long before she would starve.

And she had no magic and no way to help herself. Or her baby. Or her Sebastio. "My Goddess, help us."

"She will not come to you," Clodia shrieked. "You have broken her laws."

She didn't care. She didn't care. This wasn't right. But it was no use. All she could do was cry out, "I love you, Sebastio. Remember I love you, always."

"I love you too, Lianna. Always."

"Save our son. Make sure he knows he is loved."

"I will try." There was something wrong with Sebastio's voice, it was strained and higher. Was he going to disappear like Bastieno? "Don't leave me, Sebastio! Don't leave me!"

Clodia's laughter cackled out into the night. "You are both so pathetic and worried over the wrong things. He will not leave you. You will be the one to always leave him. But that is not enough to punish you for being chosen over me. I will make certain your love will be near but always far, never to know your love again through any of your lives," Clodia said, her voice rising into a shrill shout. "As you will never know his; never recognise him. Your forever love, your soul bond, will become as ashes on your grave as your power will become mine forever more."

The High Priestess raised her hands higher, wind whipping around her now, the cries of their baby and Sebastio drowned by the howls of the dark power that threatened to steal everything Lianna held dear.

Clodia's gaze met Lianna across the pentacle. The jewel in the necklace she wore glowed darkly red, pulsing like a heart. Lines of dark-tinged red light shot across the five points, lighting up the lines of the pentacle the High Priestess had dug into the grass.

Lianna screamed as it shot into her, but her scream was

cut off as the power squeezed around her chest, lifting her into the air. Light from the glowing pentacle blinded her.

Clodia laughed, the sound a shriek in the wind that tore at Lianna's *stola* and cut gashes in her skin as she hung above the magical inscription for elemental earth – earth that was soon to be her grave.

Clodia's mouth twisted and she cried out:

"I bind your love into my curse
You will be as a blind man dying of thirst
Reaching for that which lays so close at hand
Love slips through your fingers like grains of sand
Forever hidden from you, forever lost
Until you agree to pay the ultimate cost
I bind you and your lover into this curse
Always to be near but powerless to reverse
Animal to human, hidden from sight
Two centuries between to mourn your plight
I bind you both three times three times three
All power to me, so mote it be."

There was a roar and a flash of light as the curse hit Lianna square in the chest. It knocked her out of the pentacle and into the pit behind her. She landed with a thump, gasping for breath. Dirt started to rain down in a heavy shower; it would fill the entrance in moments. She had to move or be truly buried alive.

She tried to stand, but couldn't, so flipped over and crawled into the cell as dust filled the air around her, making it hard to breathe.

She hit a wall a few yards in. The cell was smaller than she'd thought it would be. She groped in the dark. There was supposed to be a pallet and food and water. She found the pallet but no bundle. There was no food or water. Clodia wasn't even holding properly to *Roma's* law. If the High Priest knew he would be furious. Not that he ever would know. Clodia had made certain of that, performing the ritual of live burial months before the High Priest had decreed it would be.

She wanted Lianna to die sooner rather than later, because then, and only then, could she fully take possession of Lianna's power. Then she would probably tell the High Priest Lianna had died when her child had come prematurely and she had buried her in the garden behind Vesta's Temple, as was the custom. Nobody would question the fresh mound of dirt. It was too clever. Too cruel.

But it was happening. Had happened.

Lianna sat on the thin pallet, wrapped her arms around her legs and put her forehead on her knees, trying to slow her breathing and not cough as the only entrance disappeared in a tonne of dirt. She tried to pull at the golden armbands, free herself from their binding as she'd tried to do every day since they were captured, but they refused to budge. The one good thing was that they no longer burned into her flesh. Not that it truly mattered any more because …

It was over. It was over. There was no getting out of this. Her life was over.

Her only hope was that Sebastio wouldn't meet Bastieno's fate, whatever that had been. Hoped that he would free himself soon so he could rescue their son – if he had indeed survived Clodia's spell – and take him far away from this place of despair.

She coughed, hardly able to breathe in the dusty air. She wished she could believe she'd meet them someday when her soul was reborn and they'd find their love again, but if she had it right, the curse had bound her soul so she would never know her love until ... until she'd paid the ultimate cost.

Wasn't this the ultimate cost? How could she pay another ultimate cost?

She sat there, rocking , rocking. And, in those moments that grief didn't overwhelm her for all she'd lost, she tried to figure out what the curse meant until her last moment.

The moment the air ran out.

Her eyes closed as fog and darkness followed her down, down, down ...

CHAPTER
TEN

Violetta and Tamuel came back an hour after they'd left him, and they sat down and began to plan.

They discussed many options but realised very quickly none of them would work to wake her up without endangering her.

"I can meld with her mind and see what she is seeing in there," Tamuel said after they'd sat for a long time in silence watching her.

"You can't do that. The magic will hurt her," Bas said.

"I can do it without using magic from this Realm." He pulled a small bottle from his pocket. "It's something I got a long time ago from a friend who walks between Realms. It will allow us to mind-meld with her without using our magic."

Violetta nodded. "Then do it. We need to know what is going on her head at least."

Bas was surprised Violetta didn't ask him what it was and how it worked, but like him, she was obviously filled only with concern for Jules.

Tam nodded and pocketed the bottle, gaze on Violetta. "It will be draining though, so I will need help if we want to keep on top of whatever is going on."

"If you show me how, Tomaso, I will be happy to help with that," Violetta said.

"I can help too," Bas said. He didn't care what he had to swallow, if it would help Jules, he would do it.

Tamuel shook his head. "I'm afraid that isn't possible. You need active magic for the potion to work because that's what it binds itself to. You don't have enough magic in you for it to work."

Bas glared at him. "You will both tell me exactly what she is experiencing when you go in there."

"Of course," they both said.

"Good."

He sat quietly as Tamuel talked Violetta through how to do it after having a sip of the potion, then took the first turn mind-melding with Jules.

When he came out, he was grey and there were tears in his eyes. It took him a few moments to collect himself before he could tell them what he had seen: the moments after Lianna gave birth to the moment she died. It was devastating to know that was what she was seeing; that she was living through it again. He wished she could be remembering anything else, but there was nothing he could do to change it for her.

All he could do was hold her hand and talk to her so she knew she wasn't alone.

Violetta, when she tried again later that night saw exactly the same thing. It seemed that Jules was reliving the same moment over and over again – the worst moments of Lianna's life.

And so it went for the next forty-eight hours.

Bastien sat beside Jules for those two days and nights, only leaving her side when the change took him over. Tamuel and Violetta took turns coming in to bring him food and check on Jules and spend time in Jules's vision with her. When they weren't with him and Jules, they were out trying to find the exact location the curse had been placed and for the gem they had seen Clodia wear in Jules' vision.

He hadn't remembered about the jewel and Esta hadn't written anything about it in her journal, so Jules having this vision now was the best timing, because if they didn't copy exactly what Clodia did in placing the curse, they wouldn't be able to break it. And obviously the jewel was very important.

Thankfully Tamuel recognised the gem. It was called the HeartsBlood Gem – an ancient and powerful precious stone rumoured to have been cut from the heart of an ancient Goddess. It was the reason Clodia had managed to bind Bas so he couldn't fight back. Tamuel also suspected she'd also used it to push more power into the armbands she'd put on Lianna as a child that had allowed her access to Lianna's powers. However, something had gone wrong in her use of it that night and her plan had backfired. She'd lost control of Lianna's power at her death, rather than becoming mistress of it.

The information was a double-edged sword though – they would now need the gem to help break the curse but it hadn't been seen for centuries. Thankfully Tamuel was certain he'd seen something about where it might be in the Roman Coven's library.

Bastien just hoped he was right.

Jules whimpered. He grasped her hand. It was cold. Too cold. "Come on, Jules. Wake up." He smoothed the mass of her silky curls back from her face then took a chance and kissed her forehead. Pain lanced through his eye, but he kissed her again.

The door behind him opened.

"Did you find it yet?"

"Not yet, but we will," Tamuel said.

Violetta's presence prickled over his back as she came to stand behind him. Her power felt edgier, a little less controlled than usual. But that was only to be expected, he supposed. If he still had access to his powers, he imagined they'd feel edgier too, given how worried he was about Jules. Even so, he said, "Careful with your power."

"How is she?" Violetta asked, pulling her power back.

"She's cold and struggling to breathe."

"She should wake soon then."

"She better." She might be reborn again in the future, but she wouldn't be Jules. And he loved Jules, his love for her deeper, sweeter, stronger than ever before. It killed him to think she might not love him back, but better she be alive and in love with someone else, thinking of him only as a friend, than to not be in this world at all.

He didn't want to live in a world that she did not live in. He'd had to do that too many times already, but this time, he feared, he wouldn't survive the loss.

"I think she's coming around," Violetta said. "Her lids are fluttering."

Jules sat bolt upright with a loud gasp. She tore her hand out of his, her movements frantic as she struggled to breathe.

"Jules, it's okay, you can breathe. You can breathe." He grabbed her shoulders, moving along her arms to her hands – they were at her throat, scrabbling. He pulled them away and held them.

Violetta said in a low, calm voice, "Bastien is right,

Julianna dear. You are free of the vision. Just breathe. Breathe. Focus on my voice, on Bastien's touch, and breathe. In, then out. Slow. Nice and slow. Yes, that's it. That's my girl."

Her hand brushed past him, as if she wanted to touch Jules, but she pulled away before she did. "That's a girl. That's better," she said. "Open your eyes. Can you see me?"

"Uh-huh."

"Can you see Tomaso?"

"Yes."

"And Bastien?"

Jules twisted then gasped. "You changed clothes?"

He nodded, smiling, throat too full of relief to allow him to speak, wishing more than anything that he could see more than her aura right now.

He felt her stiffen on the bed beside him as she gasped. "What is it? What's wrong?"

"How long have I been out?"

"It's the evening of the seventh."

"No!" She jerked, her hands twisting out of his grip. "I've lost two days?"

"Shh, shh," Violetta said. "You must stay calm."

She didn't – her agitation and distress were hot jabs against his skin. He pulled her to him, tucking her head under his chin, hand stroking over her back. She felt too thin – the vision had taken too much out of her. "It's not lost," he whispered against the crinkling curls of her hair that tickled his chin. "We know so much more now. It has helped. Your vision has helped."

Slowly, she began to soften in his hold, her breath slowing and deepening.

"She died. Lianna. So lost and alone."

The heartache in her voice made him want to weep. "I

know." He cupped her face and lifted it up, pressed his lips against her forehead again despite the pain it caused him. "But she's not alone now. We're all here."

"That's right," Tamuel said. "And we're going to put an end to this. And then you can be with your love. You just have to believe."

"Yes." She didn't sound too thrilled. She swallowed hard, pulled back a little. He let go of her but she gripped his hands, held on. "I couldn't see him. I still don't know who he is."

"That's okay," Tamuel said. "I—"

Bastien said quickly, "We can cover all of what we have discovered after we get some food into Jules. You must be starving."

She nodded slowly. "I am hungry."

"Then let's go get you something to eat. The rest can wait."

At least, it had to, until she'd had a chance to recover. Right now, she felt too much like she might slip away from him.

CHAPTER
ELEVEN

Jules stared at the map of the Forum that Tomaso had spread out in the middle of the table in front of her until Tomaso placed a large bowl of delicious smelling Puttanesca pasta in front of her.

She was still feeling a bit disoriented from losing two days with nightmares – no, not nightmares, memories – swirling around in her mind like a chaotic maelstrom.

But that disorientation didn't affect her hunger.

She was ravenous.

Without waiting, she picked up her fork and dove in, almost moaning at the delicious flavours of tomato, basil and the saltiness of anchovies and olives burst to life on her tongue. "This is delicious," she said around a mouthful.

"Yes it is," Bas said as he twisted more pasta onto his fork. "Thank you, my friend."

"It's good to see you eating properly again," Tomaso said.

Jules turned to Bas. "You've not been eating?"

"I have eaten," he said gesturing with his spaghetti-laden fork before putting it into his mouth.

"Not much," Tomaso said wryly as he cut up some fresh bread. "I took away almost as much food as I brought up to you."

"Bas! You should have looked after yourself better than that."

"Jules is right," Tomaso said, sitting down to pick up us own fork. "You look like a bag of bones!"

"I promise to make up for my lack of eating now," he said before putting another heaped forkful of pasta in his mouth.

She watched him for a moment to make certain he kept eating before returning to her food.

They ate in silence for long moments, only the sound of forks against the plates and the distant noises of the city filling the air.

Until Tomaso cleared his throat. She looked up at him.

"Jules, I want to apologise for what happened."

"You don't need to do th—"

"I do," he said, holding up his hand. "Even though I thought I had my magic suppressed sufficiently and had no idea just shaking your bare hand could push you into a vision, I shouldn't have given into the urge. I am old enough to know better. I didn't mean to put you through that."

"I'm glad you did," she said around a mouthful of delicious salty spaghetti *Puttanesca*. "Otherwise, you wouldn't have found out about the HeartsBlood Gem. You think you can find it?"

He nodded. "The books in the Roman Coven I tracked down all say it's rumoured to be buried somewhere in *Roma*, although nobody's been able to figure out where – which is strange given the magical signature it should give off. But now we know Clodia used it in her spell to help hold Sebastio and Lianna and leach their powers, I think I'll be able to recalibrate the magical signature and track it down."

"It could be anywhere in Rome," Violetta said as she placed a bowl of salad on the table and sat down. "It's a long shot to think we'll find it."

"I don't think so," Jules said.

They all turned to look at her and she waved her hand. "Given how Clodia used it, the gem would be tied to the area where the spell was cast." They kept staring at her. "Am I the only one here who's read Varagustus' *Treatise on the Properties of Powerful Stones*?"

"I think you're the only one ever to read Varagustus' treatises on anything," Tomaso said dryly. "The man's style is boring enough to put you to sleep. Not to mention all his treatises are thousands of pages long. And most of them are written in a lost language."

"Not lost," she said. "I understood it."

"What did it say?" Bastien asked her.

She took a sip of water, ordering her thoughts. "Gems like that need a link to someone or something with ties to the Gods. I don't think the link was made to Clodia given her spell backfired."

"Of course," Tomaso said. "The link was made with the place, and to a smaller extent, Lianna and Sebastio." He pointed to the Temple of Vesta on the map in front of them. "It must be somewhere here, close to wherever the curse was cast."

"This is fantastic," Bastien said.

"Really?" she asked. "But we'll need to use magic to find it and," she waved her hand at herself, "you can't do that when we're down there looking for the curse-spot."

"We don't have to wait until night to find it," Tomaso said. "I can start to look for it during the day when I can use my magic without it affecting you. I'll find it. I promise."

She nodded, managed a smile. Somehow, despite what touching him had done to her, she couldn't help but like and trust him. She supposed it was because Violetta and Bastien did. And he seemed to have so much knowledge about all sorts of things – even if he thought Varagustus' fascinating writings boring.

She finished the last mouthful of her pasta, wiped up the sauce with a piece of crusty bread so she could enjoy every last morsel of the delicious meal. She then drank down another glass of water before saying. "So, what's next?"

Tomaso let out a loud breath. "I want you to look at this map and see if there's anything familiar to you. It might help us to pinpoint where to look if there is."

Jules stared at the yellowing map once again. It was old and had a stain in one corner and showed details that the maps the tourists were given of the ancient ruins didn't have. She wondered where it had come from. And if there was a trick to reading it that she just wasn't getting.

She was about to ask him when the voice interrupted her.

"It just looks like lines and squares and squiggles."

"I know."

"We're not very good with maps."

"I know."

She stared hard at it, trying to see something that might trigger a memory of her time as Lianna. Nothing came. She made a sound of frustration. "I'm sorry. This doesn't look familiar at all."

"It's all right, dearest," Violetta said. "We don't expect you to know much of anything."

91

"What? Why?" Her gaze jerked to Violetta. Did her grandmama have such little faith in her?

Violetta waved her hand. "The curse, of course. Its purpose is to actively stop you from doing anything that might break it."

"Oh ... of course." Her shoulders slumped. "So, I'm virtually useless."

"Not at all," Tomaso and Bas said together.

"You're the only one who can find the place the curse was cast," Tomaso said. "You're vital to the success of our endeavour."

"What about the pentacle?" Bas asked, frowning Violetta's way. "Surely that left some magical trace – it was so strong."

Violetta nodded as she and Tomaso shared a look. "From what we saw in your vision, it looked like it was burned up in the final burst of power. Even if it wasn't, the strongest magic would barely register after all these years. You would have to be a super-sensitive to find it."

Jules jerked upright from her slump. "I am." They all turned to stare at her. "What you said about the sensitive thing. I'm that. Maybe not in how you meant, but my allergy to magic makes me super sensitive to it. I might pick something up that you are all missing."

Bas stilled beside her. "That might be what Esta referred to – about Lianna's soul finding the place. Perhaps she guessed the curse would make Lianna's reincarnations allergic to magic."

"That's a supposition. I don't remember her being certain of anything of the sort," Violetta said carefully.

"But it makes sense." Bas stood. "We have to get down there and check it out."

"Julianna has only just recovered from her vision.

92

Perhaps we should wait until tomorrow night," Violetta said, her concerned gaze on Jules.

"I want to do this," Jules said, pushing her chair back and standing. "I might not be able to help track down the HeartsBlood Gem, and I can't help with finding the lover—"

"That's what I tried to tell you before," Tomaso interrupted. "I did an invocation spell when Violetta called to say this was happening. It took a few tries, but I eventually found this Sebastio. I have contacted him and he is excited to be able to meet you ... again."

"When is he coming?"

"Not until just before midnight on Valentine's Eve. He can't reveal himself until then because of the curse."

She nodded, relieved Tomaso's knowledge extended to knowing God invocation spells – she'd have to ask him about that one day. But for now ... "The only thing I can do is go to the Forum and find where the spell was cast. So let's go."

"We should wait until midnight – it's quietest then." Tomaso looked her up and down. "That will give you time to shower and change. You'll need to dress warmly. It's cold outside."

CHAPTER
TWELVE

It was dark as they left the *pensione*, the moon mostly obscured by clouds and the few street lights not shining very brightly.

Usually panic would start to rise as they walked down the narrow streets, the old buildings rising above her in a way that made it seem like they were leaning in. But she only experienced the apprehension she'd had ever since waking to discover she'd put them back two days. And the natural worry about whether she could do this; find the exact place the curse was cast.

Maybe the lack of extreme panic she normally experienced in the darkness was because these streets seemed familiar – she must have walked these streets often when she'd been Lianna. Or did it have more to do with the man walking at her side, his hand lightly on her arm as she helped him navigate the cobbled streets?

Bells clanged, announcing it was midnight – the seventh day passing into the eighth – as they followed Tomaso through a maze of streets that were curiously empty. Their footsteps echoed in the air around them, sounding lonely and a bit lost.

But Tomaso wasn't lost and finally they emerged onto the *Via del Corso*, crossed the *Piazza Venezia* and then made their way down the *Via dei Fori Imperiali*. A few cars and trucks still rattled along the thoroughfare – Rome never truly slept – but it was nowhere near the chaos and cacophony that had deafened – and terrified – her on the crazy taxi ride from the airport to Tomaso's villa three days ago.

They walked silently and quickly down the wide *Via dei Fori Imperiali* towards the Colosseum and the Forum, which lay in ruins beside the behemoth. The Colosseum glowed, dressed in light from the moon and the spotlights on the grounds surrounding it.

"*Even in ruins, it is still a colossus,*" the voice whispered pensively.

"*It is. And the history in those stones ...*"

"*It's loud.*"

"*Uh-huh.*"

She shuddered as something inside her curled into itself. Her skin prickled and crawled uncomfortably, like it did when someone was using magic nearby.

But there was nobody around except for her and her companions and none of them would use magic around her, so it couldn't be that. Still, she had to fight the need to turn and run – far, far away.

"You okay?" Bastien whispered, leaning down so his warm breath brushed her ear.

She took a deep breath, edging closer to him. "I'm fine."

"*Not true.*"

"*It's not not true.*"

"*You know you're not making sense?*"

Tomaso turned. "Come. I've placed a spell to keep the security cameras and guards away for a time. It shouldn't affect you at all because it's not in the air, but more like a virus I placed on the guards and the electronics," he said to Jules, "So don't worry."

She wasn't – she was more worried about what was happening to her right now. She glanced around but still saw nobody near them – and to feel like this, someone would need to be using magic close by.

As they drew closer to the ancient ruins, the prickling increased. As did the shouting of long-dead crowds, the ancient cries of the enslaved and the roars of the animals kept inside for the amusement of the Roman people. The noise surrounded her, pushing at her. Her stomach roiled, her heart beat faster.

They stopped at the edge of the road opposite the Colosseum. The concourse that ran around it stretched in front of her, wavering. Was it moving or was she moving? She wished whatever it was would stop expanding and contracting like that. She was going to be sick.

She had to force herself to keep breathing evenly, to not wrap her fingers tightly around Bastien's arm. He was the only thing that felt real. The only thing keeping her from running away, screaming from the force of history pounding at her from the structure in front of them – because that's what this had to be. She wasn't just sensitive to magic, but to the impact of it through history.

"No point standing here," Violetta said. "Let's go."

They stepped off the curb together and walked quickly across the road. And every step she had to push herself harder and harder to keep going. By the time they reached the opposite side, she was panting – and not from the short run across the road. She was clinging to Bas now harder than he held onto her.

"Are you okay, Jules?" he asked quietly.

"Fine," she managed through clenched teeth and took the final step up the curb and onto the concourse.

The moment her foot touched the ancient paving, history came crashing down on her. She stumbled under its weight, losing her grip on Bastien.

Emotion – terror, elation – vibrated up through her feet. Her heart raced, her skin prickled so it almost hurt. The need to flee was a shout in every nerve.

"Are you all right, dearest? You don't look very well."

"I don't feel very well." The words were slurred, uncertain.

"Jules."

"What's wrong?"

She tried to form words, but pitched forward, landing on her hands and knees, and vomited her dinner all over the stones.

The world span faster. And alongside the spinning, pain began to make itself known. It filled her head alongside the roars and screams.

She couldn't do it. She couldn't go any further. It was too much. Too much.

"Shit," she heard someone say, then arms were around her and she was lifted and carried away.

BAS WAS CHAFING to get back to Jules, but he forced himself to finish the plate of food that had been placed before him a few minutes ago.

The change had taken so much longer than ever before

and it had wiped him out for an hour afterwards. Then Violetta wouldn't allow him to return to Jules – she actually closed the bedroom door, locking him out! – until he'd eaten the breakfast Tamuel had made for him.

The only reason he was managing to swallow it down was because Jules had been worried about him not eating. He didn't want to give her reason to worry about him when she eventually woke up. So he ate, glaring at the two worry-warts who stood over him.

But as soon as he finished, he turned, and, giving Tamuel his cat death-stare over his shoulder, spoke to him mind-to mind – they'd discovered some years ago he was able to communicate like this with the cupid in his cat form. *"Open her door now. I want to check on her. She's been alone too long."* He began to trot towards the stairs.

Tamuel groaned and said, "Hang on. There's some things I need to tell you."

"Tell me in her room." He kept going.

"Bastien, no!" Violetta's command snapped through the air at the same time a barrier rose before him, cutting off access to the stairs.

He hissed, his hackles raising as he swung around. He wanted to swipe at the old woman, hurt her in some way like she was hurting him.

But then he saw her face and his rage flew away. Hanging his head, he meowed piteously.

She came over to him, crouched down, and stroked his head. "I understand, my friend. You need to be with her. The curse has never done away with that need, has it?"

He shook his head.

"That's good."

His head snapped up to look at her. If he could frown at

98

her, he would, but instead he could only make an enquiring meow.

Tamuel seemed a little shocked too, because he said, "You think it's good that he experiences the pain of unrequited love?"

She smiled crookedly at Bas as she rose to her feet smoothly. "I didn't mean that as it sounded. I meant that it is good he has such strong instincts to look after Jules. She needs to be cared for now more than ever. It's going to be even more important that she feels supported in that way to get her through what is to come."

"And what is to come?" Tamuel asked for him.

She looked away, staring out of the window that faced the direction the Forum was in. "Terrible hardship and pain. You think last night was a one-off? That she only got knocked out by the memories that hit her because she was unprepared?"

"Well, I was kind of hoping that was the case," Tamuel said. Bas meowed his agreement.

Violetta shook her head sadly, still looking away. "You are foolish then." She pointed at Bas. "There is a reason your changes are getting harder. And there's a reason why Jules had such a severe reaction to returning to the place she spent so much time in when she was Lianna. The curse. It's fighting against you. I was afraid of this." She sighed heavily as she turned back to face them. "Things are only going to get harder. I am afraid it is going to take more than Jules is going to be able to endure to get the information we need."

Bas shook his head. *"No. She will do it. She is strong. Stronger than anyone knows."*

Tamuel repeated his words to Violetta. She bent down and cupped his face. "I know she is strong, Bastien. I have always known just how strong she is. But it isn't our belief that counts here. It's hers. And I'm not sure she has enough belief in herself to get through this."

"What can we do?" Tamuel asked.

She stood and gestured down at Bas again. "I think the only one who can truly help her is Bas. Your love for her might be the only thing that will help her now. Which is why I said it was good he feels the way he does."

"But he can't tell her he loves her," Tamuel said.

"He has to find a way. And failing that, he has to do everything he can to show her what he feels even if it causes him terrible pain. Even if it drains him further. Because it is not Bas at this point who can help us with what we need. It's Jules. We need her to get to the Forum. We need her to remember. And we can't afford for her to completely collapse like she did last night."

Violetta was right. They couldn't afford many more delays. She was also right that he wasn't important. Only Jules was important. He nodded at her, saying to Tamuel. *"I will do everything I can to make sure she knows I believe in her and that I love her."*

"Good," Violetta said after Tamuel had repeated his words. She waved her hand. "You can go up to her then. Tomaso and I will be out and about today, but we will make sure one or the other comes back to regularly check on her and one of us will be here to sit with her while you go through your change later today."

"You're looking for the gem?" Bas asked Tamuel.

He nodded. "We are. I think we have just the spell to help us pinpoint it. We probably won't be able to collect it until tonight, but we can try to figure out exactly where it is today."

"Good luck," Bas said, then turned and ran up the stairs.

"Tamuel, can you open the door for him? My knees really don't need to climb those stairs again."

Tamuel didn't hurry as much as Bas would have liked. Bas was growling low in his throat by the time the cupid joined him and opened the door.

He didn't bother saying thank you or goodbye, but just raced into the room to jump up on Jules' bed.

She was so pale and still, the only movement were her eyes flicking back and forth under her eyelids indicating she was dreaming vividly - no not dreaming. Having memories. Lianna's memories.

He hoped his old lover was sharing something far more pleasant than what she'd shared last time this had happened. But as he sat and watched her, a frown appeared between her brows and her face drew tight with tension and he knew the memories she was experiencing were as bad as the ones she'd had before.

He wished he could comfort her, talk to her, hold her. But in his cat form all he could do was curl up next to her and purr deeply, hoping the softness of his fur against her arm and the vibrations of his purr reached her where she was, lost in memories of a woman who lived thousands of years ago and gave her the comfort they usually did.

And hope that maybe she saw something else that would help them.

While he lay there with her, hoping, he filled himself with the love he felt for her, and despite the pain thinking of that love always brought to him, he pushed it out of himself and into her, endeavouring to imbue his touch, his purr, with all the love he felt for her.

CHAPTER
THIRTEEN

Jules came to slowly, the softness under her head and body telling her she was on a bed. She opened her eyes to be greeted by semi-darkness – a nightlight had been left on to the side of the bed, lighting the room enough to know this was her bedroom at the *pensione*. The amount of light it shed wasn't as good as the nightlight she had in her room at home, but it was enough light for the fear to not truly raise its head.

In fact, the fear of the dark didn't seem to be as bad as it had been. Maybe it was because she now knew the true source of her fear – the fact she'd been buried alive in a small room, dying alone in the dark, dust closing in all around her, clogging her lungs. This was not that. Nothing would be like that. She was safe here – she knew she was safe here – so there was no true reason to worry.

But Hells, her head felt like it was full of wet sand, her eyes equally so. What the Hells had happened?

"You passed out."

"Again?"

"Yes. The history in the stones—"

102

"It overwhelmed me. Gods-damned curse."

"You said it."

She wondered how long she'd been out. She had no idea if she'd lost more days or not. She needed her phone. It was there on the bedside table – she could see its outline in the glow from the nightlight.

She shifted but couldn't move. A warm weight lay over her waist, warmth aligned along her side – Bastien curled up beside her, his arm over her stomach. She craned to look at him, the light enabling her to see he was still fully dressed and dark shadows marked the skin under his eyes.

She didn't want to wake him – he'd obviously had very little sleep. But she wanted to know how much time she'd lost. The fact he was still in his human form told her it couldn't be more than a few hours, but still, she needed to check. If there was enough time, she'd like to go back and try again.

She moved carefully, edged forward, enough to grip her phone with her fingertips, then pulled it towards her until she could pick it up.

She pressed her thumb on the home button to light up the screen.

The date lit up with the time:

4:05 am.

10 February.

She jerked upright, clutching her phone.

Beside her, Bastien came to a crouch, hands lifted. "What is it? What's wrong? Who's there?"

"I've lost another *two days!*" She turned her phone off then on again, but the date didn't change. They'd gone to the Colosseum at midnight just as it tipped into the eighth and now it was the tenth? "Fuck."

"It's okay." Bastien came down beside her to hug her.

"We've got time. And you did so great. You'll do better next time."

She wanted to give in to his comforting warmth, but instead, pushed away to stand and pace. "I did great?" She snorted. "If you call throwing up and passing out for another two days 'great', then I guess I'm the champ at that."

"Don't, Jules. Don't blame yourself," Bastien said softly from behind her. "You're not to blame for how the curse affects you."

"Then who is?"

"Clodia."

"Well, good luck blaming her – she's dead."

"Yeah, and a part of me wishes she wasn't so that I could make her pay for doing what she did to us just so she could steal and use Goddess-gifted powers that weren't hers."

"Goddess-gifted powers?" Had she known that? Yes, she thought perhaps she did remember that her powers had been Goddess-gifted. It was difficult at times to keep things straight within that swirl of Lianna's memories that filled her mind. And there was also the fact the curse didn't like her thinking about it too much – it hurt so much when she did. But ... "How are you able to tell me that?" Gasping, she turned to grab his arm. "No. Don't answer that."

His mouth curled into a gentle smile. "It's okay. I can talk about Clodia and my opinions about her. The curse only stops me from talking about Lianna—" He winced. "Talking about how much I lo—" He jerked this time, the wince louder.

"Don't. Please don't hurt yourself by talking about—" Pain slid along her veins, making her stop before she finished the sentence.

"Jules?" he asked, voice still tight with the pain he obviously felt.

"I'm fine. I stopped in time." She brushed trembling fingers over his brow. She hated that he could hurt like this because of her. "Maybe just tell me what you remember of Clodia. Nothing else."

He swallowed hard, nodded, then said carefully, "Clodia was not Vesta's chosen vessel for her most cherished power and she hated that fact. She was sent a vision about who it would be given to, which is how she came to be there to take you from your parents the moment you were born."

"But ... hang on. I didn't think Vestal Virgins were chosen until they were at least six."

"Not usually. But you were an exception because you were Goddess-blessed."

She wished people would stop talking as if she and Lianna were the same person – they weren't, even though Lianna had been with her all these years, a presence in her head, talking to her. So she just said, "My dreams ... visions – they never showed me that. Her parents? They just happily gave her away?"

"I don't know about that. I do know your family always birthed strong witches. Which is how Esta came to be chosen too. She was your – Lianna's – cousin."

She knew Esta was a distant relation of theirs – otherwise, she wouldn't have been reincarnated in Violetta – but for some reasons she'd never truly thought about the significance of the fact that Lianna and Esta were related and what it must have been like for the young novice to lose Lianna like that. "She must have been very powerful for Clodia to pull her into the pentacle the way she did."

"She was, but Lianna was more so. Her power frightened Clodia. I think that infuriated her. It also made her insanely jealous. Nobody realised how much until—"

His mouth pulled tight. They were obviously skating close to the edge of what he could and couldn't tell her. She had to move the conversation back to just Clodia. "Tomaso mentioned her spell must have gone wrong. Why? How?"

He frowned. "That's a great question."

"Yes, it is."

"Thank you."

"We always knew she never got your power—"

"Lianna's power," she said cautiously. There was no flash of pain from the curse, so she assumed this was something they were allowed to talk about. "I don't have any power. Not like her."

Bastien's brow furrowed deeply. "Despite the fact she was a trained witch, she never had access to her full powers either. Clodia channelled them and used them for her purposes as High Priestess from when Lianna was young. If Clodia had gotten full control of them, they would have made her virtually immortal. But she died soon after the casting."

"But something must have gone right," Jules said. "Because her curse has lasted all these years."

"Yes."

She rubbed the ache in her brow that was steadily growing stronger as they spoke. "What I don't understand is where did the power go? If Clodia didn't get it and Lianna didn't get access to it to stop herself from dying – and I certainly don't have it – where is it?"

"I don't know. I've never ..." His frown deepened. "You should discuss this with Tomaso and Violetta in the morning."

"After you recover from your change."

106

"Yes. After that."

Silence fell between them. There was something she wanted to ask him, but she was afraid it would hurt him.

"Ask me."

"What?" Jules picked at a hangnail.

"You want to ask what power Lianna ... had?" He swallowed hard.

"How did he know?"

"He knows you incredibly well."

"You don't have to tell me. Not if it hurts you—"

"She had the power to light a fire in hearts and hearths," he said quickly but showed no sign of pain.

"It doesn't sound like much, does it?"

She screwed up her nose – she had to agree. "That doesn't seem worth going to this much effort over."

"Are you kidding?" He turned to her, his face alight with an energy she'd not seen in him before, a lightness. "The power to change a man's heart and therefore his thoughts through the power of your very presence. It's influence incarnate. Something that could shape nations. It's the only thing worth this much effort. That and ... love." The last word was choked and his hands spasmed on hers.

"Don't." She put her hand over his mouth, his soft, full lips warm against her palm. "Don't hurt yourself. Not for me. Not for this."

He shook his head. "No. I'm fine. I shouldn't have—" He swallowed, paling a little, his eyelid flickering.

"Bastien, stop it." She clasped his face in both hands, her thumbs stroking his cheeks. "You know I hate it when you're hurting."

"So you know how I feel when you hurt."

Her mind skipped sideways in a way that made her feel slightly sick. "Yeah, well ... Clodia. Total bitch, right?"

He snort-laughed, his eyes crinkling in that way she liked. "Right. I never—"

His words choked off as he spasmed out of her grasp and flipped off the bed.

"Bastien!" She threw herself down beside him, hardly noting the smart in her knees above the panic rising in her chest, squeezing her breath. "Bastien, stop thinking about it."

"I'm ... not," he squeezed out. "Change. Cat."

"What? No." Dawn wasn't for hours given it was still winter. He shouldn't be changing. But he was.

And he'd never make it to his changing booth in his room down the hall.

"Run ... away," he said in an agonised whisper.

"No, no," she pleaded. "It's not time."

"Do what he says. Now! It could kill us if we're here when he changes."

"But he's in so much pain."

"We can't help him. Not with this. Not yet. Just go. Run!"

Her stomach turned over and her heart clenched in her chest as the power of his change radiated outwards. She scrambled backwards before the strength of it could touch her, fumbling with the door handle before managing to push it down and open the door. She stumbled out of the room, slamming the door shut before staggering down the hall, trying to get away from the magic that whipped at her, making her bleed, sobbing because of the need to leave her best friend to endure this horrible pain alone.

She made it down the stairs, holding herself upright by sheer force of will and a good grip on the banister, but could go no more than two steps beyond the bottom of the stairs. She leaned against the wall, then slid down it, the cold of the tiles under her bottom a relief to the burning that raced through the rest of her body. She wanted to cry, to sob, to scream and yell, but she couldn't. She had to think. Think.

She'd thought that being bound to a curse because of a love that had never been hers and then losing days because of it was bad enough. But this was a potential disaster because his early change the other night hadn't been a fluke.

"Has he changed earlier on the days you were unconscious?"

"I don't know!"

She'd noticed at Christmas that his changes were taking longer; taking more of a toll, but not to this extent. He'd changed every sunset and sunrise for thousands of years, so what had changed the pattern?

"You."

"What?"

"This started when you found out about the curse."

"Fuck."

CHAPTER
FOURTEEN

Power crackled in the air as Bastien twisted and jerked, his body breaking and reshaping one bone, one ligament at a time. It had taken him completely by surprise and he couldn't hold back the scream that tore out of his mouth.

All he could be thankful for was that Jules had managed to get out of the room. He only hoped she'd made it further, because, given he wasn't in the shielding of his portable changing booth, the magic of the spell would hurt her if she wasn't at least outside.

The door banged open, crashing against the plaster with a loud crack. Then hands were on him – Tamuel. "Where ... Jules," he managed to say.

"Safe." The cupid picked him up and carried him down the hall to his booth, shutting the door. It closed with a whoosh and a pop as the magical shield that kept the power of the spell inside the booth, automatically fell into place. Violetta's spellwork was quite ingenious.

"Thank you," he mouthed to his friend as he stood

outside the booth, arms crossed, worry deep lines on his face.

Then all thought departed as his lungs, ribs and spine twisted and reshaped and everything was lost in the agony of the change.

An endless time later, he rolled over and groaned, the sound coming out as a squashed meow. Everything hurt, more than he'd ever remembered it hurting after a change.

It had worsened every night since Jules had found out about the curse. And his time as a human was now down to seven hours.

This was not good.

His stomach groaned and gurgled as the scent of bacon wafted under his nose and he realised just how hungry he was. And thirsty. His tongue felt like a dried leaf stuck to the roof of his mouth.

He pushed upright gingerly, surprised to realise he was on the bed. Jules must have put him here after his change was complete and the shield that protected her had disabled itself. She always saw to his comfort. She'd also placed a bowl of water on the bedside table right next to him.

As he drank his fill, he slowly became aware of the light in the room. Light not from the bulb above him but shining through the window.

Hells. How long had he been out? He needed to find Jules and the others.

He jumped down and padded across to the door, glad it had been left ajar. He slipped out into the hallway, picked up Jules's scent – vanilla, cinnamon and spice with a hint of pine – and followed it down the stairs, past the lounge, through the kitchen and out into the private walled courtyard. Her scent angled towards the ivy-covered arches that led to the little garden area.

Typical she'd be out here, even with how cold it was. She loved spending time outdoors, seeking the sun and light whenever she took a break from her work in the library. She and Lianna shared that in common.

He winced at the lash of pain that was punishment for that thought, shook his head, and continued through the archway.

The three of them sat at a small table in an alcove to the left in the only area of the garden that caught the sun in winter. Water trickled down the wall and into a small pond where huge gold and white speckled goldfish swam – he was almost hungry enough to hook his paw in and fish one of them out. But he smelled bacon again. Spotted a plate piled high in the middle of the table. Thank the Gods.

Jules looked up, a smile brightening her face. "Bastien." She patted the table beside her. His stomach rumbled as he leaped up. "You haven't eaten? I left food for you in our room."

"He wanted to know where you were first."

She glanced at Tamuel. "You can hear him?"

"You can't tell her about our cupid-link."

Tamuel shot him a quick look as if to say 'duh' before smiling and saying, "I have a talent for talking to animals. Just call me Doctor Doolittle."

"Oh." She swallowed hard. "I'm glad someone can hear him." She pulled the plate of bacon to sit in front of him and began to cut it into cat-bite-sized pieces. "Eat. Now."

He did. Voraciously.

"Better?" Jules said, stroking her hand down his back with a smile as he finished the plate a few minutes later.

He nodded, even though he was still a little hungry. Not

surprising given the change took more out of him and was more vicious than ever before. A shiver chased down his spine. He didn't want to think about what that meant right now.

"You should think about it," Tamuel said.

"It's not important."

"I beg to differ."

Bastien shook his head at the argumentative cupid. *"The only thing we should be worried about is getting Jules through the trials the curse is throwing in her path to stop her from breaking it. What is happening to me is inconsequential."*

"It won't be inconsequential if you can't take your human form on Valentine's Eve."

"What is he saying?" Jules sat forward, hands clasped before her, face drawn and pale, but otherwise seemingly unhurt. She'd got away just in time, or Tamuel had got him into his booth before it was too late.

There were dark circles under her eyes though. Had she slept at all after he changed last night?

Tamuel turned to glare at him. "He doesn't think it matters that he's spending less and less time as a human and the change is sucking his remaining power and energy from him."

"Bastien." Jules glowered at him. "Of course it matters. Grandmama and Tomaso are worried that unless you're in the form you were in when the curse was cast, it won't break."

"You're focused on the wrong thing."

Her gaze whipped from Tamuel after he related Bastien's words, and back to him. "Really? The fact you might not be able to hold your human form when the time comes doesn't worry you?"

"Of course it worries me. But only breaking the curse can

change it. Worrying is only going to stop you from doing what you must. Besides, I think this is another way the curse has of stopping us from reaching our goal. I think the more you worry on it, the worse it will get because it means it's winning."

"That makes no sense," Jules said as Tamuel finished translating. "Why would the curse suddenly change after all this time? For you and for me? I mean, how does it know we're here and trying to break it? Why is it suddenly upping the ante? I know I'm not an expert on magic, but I didn't think a spell could have sentience unless the witch or wizard who cast it was alive to mould it?"

"Not usually," Violetta said, her eyes shadowed with worry. "But this is not a usual curse. It's something I brought to their attention the other night when you were unconscious and they've come to believe I am right." She shook her head. "But that's neither here-nor-there right now."

"Then what is?" Jules asked impatiently.

"The fact that Bastien's right. We must concentrate on the things we can control. You need to focus on how to get into the Forum without passing out. If you can't do that, nothing else matters, does it?"

Jules made a small sound, like a whimper. Bastien put his paw on her hand to comfort her, shooting daggers at Violetta for lumping everything on Jules's shoulders. He knew she valued speaking the truth, but didn't she realise how her blunt speech affected her granddaughter? Especially now. He'd have to have words with her later.

Or maybe Tamuel could say something to her now. He glanced at his friend, saw the glint in his eyes as he looked between Jules and Bastien. *"What is it? What have you thought of?"*

"Jules is right – the curse is acting curiously. Also, it's

strange that it is growing more powerful and not less. It makes me wonder what's at the heart of its power source."

Violetta sat forward. "Power source? That would be Clodia wouldn't it – ah." She sat back, expression wondering. "I never thought of that."

"Never thought of what?" Jules asked.

"The source of power after all this time. Curse lore states that a curse must have a power source – usually that of the witch or wizard who spelled it."

Tamuel nodded. "That's right. But no magical being alone is strong enough to power a curse for this long unless they have progeny to tie into powering their spellwork, and even then, it couldn't be maintained at this level of strength. I've often wondered what kept it going through the ages."

Jules nodded. "Wouldn't the HeartsBlood Gem have something to do with that?"

Tamuel paused, eyebrows screwing up in thought. "Maybe. But only if added to an active power source. And only if it was kept near that power source."

"Well, we think it was kept near the pentacle, don't we?"

"The pentacle lost most of its power in the casting, so no. That wouldn't be it."

"*Didn't Esta write in her journal that she thought Clodia channelled into the power of her Goddess to bind the curse?*"

"You never mentioned feeling the Goddess Vesta there," Tamuel said, brows raising at him in surprise.

"*I didn't.*"

"What is he saying?"

Tamuel told them what Bastien had said, then followed it with, "But that is pure speculation on the young Vestal

Virgin's part because there was no evidence that the Goddess Vesta appeared at all."

"Of course she didn't. Vesta never manifested. She was a Goddess hidden in time and mystery." Jules said. "I've done a lot of research on all the pantheons over the years, and Vesta remained one of the most mysterious and secret. In fact, unlike many other Gods and Goddesses, there was no statue or bust of her in any of her forms. But her lack of manifestation is hardly proof she wasn't there. She could have just reached through her High Priestess to place the curse, thereby ensuring it would be powered for eternity."

"Ah, but," Tamuel raised his finger. "Gods and Goddesses are powered by those who worship them and Vesta no longer has followers. So even if she did help Clodia – which is by no means certain – she would not have enough power now to make the curse stronger and act like it is."

Jules sucked in a breath and chewed on her lip, her brow furrowed in that way she had when she listened to something interesting. Nodding slowly, she said, "That's true, but ... isn't she just one face of the ultimate Goddess of the Hearth and Home? The curse would be powered by her connection to that source because we still worship many various faces of that Goddess."

"She has a point."

"True," Tamuel nodded. "But each manifestation could only exist as part of the whole, with worshippers powering them through belief. Without worshippers, there is no power to tether her to the essential power that is the source of all Gods and Goddesses – the Eternal Well." He waved his hands. "And while this discussion is fascinating, we're off track. What I was trying to say is that I'm certain now that the curse is powered by the magic locked inside of you, Jules."

Violetta's eyes widened. "Of course. That's where it went."

"What?" Jules asked her.

"Your power. It never went into Clodia as she designed. It somehow got locked inside you. It has been powering the curse all this time."

"But why does it react so violently against any outward source of power?"

Tamuel shrugged. "Perhaps it's trying to protect her from more tampering?"

"That doesn't make sense. Why would it hurt her?"

"I guess the powers being Goddess-touched has something to do with it. Clodia got away with using them while Lianna was alive because she didn't try to wrest them from their seat – Lianna's soul. Then she tried to use the Hearts-Blood Gem to bind Lianna's power and aid in the transference, but it too is Goddess-touched.

"That power is not meant for anyone but those who have been gifted with it. I guess, the amplification of the two together created a backlash that warped the spell and forced the powers deep inside Lianna's soul. Unfortunately, because the HeartsBlood Gem had been used in part to bind the curse to Lianna and Sebastio, it got tied into the powers now locked inside Lianna. That's why she doesn't have access to her powers – they're caught in a loop of protecting her from possible tampering by external magical forces but also powering the curse."

Bastien stilled, gaze snapping to Jules. She was trembling. He wanted to comfort her, but she looked like she would break at the merest touch. *"Why have we never realised this before?"*

Tamuel shrugged. "You couldn't remember many of the specifics and we didn't have Violetta's memories or Jules's visions to give us the missing pieces of information."

"But what does this mean?"

"It means it's my fault," Jules said as Tamuel finished his translation, topaz eyes wide, face pale. "That I could somehow stop it if I wasn't so weak." She pushed back from the table, her chair clattering to the cobbles.

"No. No, that's not what I'm saying at all," Tamuel said.

"Jules," Bastien cried out, the sound leaving his lips as a strangled meow as she turned and took off.

Bastien raced after her, but she slammed the door shut behind her and he couldn't get out. By the time Tamuel wrenched the door open, Jules was nowhere to be seen.

Bastien swore, his cat mouth making excellent work of the sounds, but none of it helped. *"I have to find her."*

"We will. But you can't do it like that. Stay here. I'll go."

"Neither of you are going anywhere," Violetta said, joining them at the door. "Jules will be back."

"How can you be so certain?" Tamuel repeated Bastien's question for Violetta.

"I know my granddaughter. No matter how upset she is right now, no matter how much she might want to give up, she won't. She'll be back because she longs to be loved and because she needs to save you." With that, she turned back inside. "Come on, you two. No point standing there gaping at the empty street. We've got a lot of work to do to prepare for tonight. We've only got three more nights to get this right."

CHAPTER
FIFTEEN

J ules tore down the cobbled street, through a plaza
and into another, weaving in and out of the crowds of
sightseers and locals celebrating *Carnevale.*

It was too much. All of it – too much.

She was bound to a curse because of a power she had no
access to. She was bound to a curse because of a love she'd
never felt. She was bound to a curse because an ancient
Coven-leader-High-Priestess-bitch-witch had coveted
something that wasn't hers.

And because of all of that, her best friend had been
dragged into the mess with her.

Or more to the point, he was Lianna's best friend. He
only stayed around her because of Lianna.

She was getting the dregs of Lianna's life – including
her lover.

"You want to be loved."

"Not if he doesn't love me for me."

"But he loves Lianna and you are Lianna."

"No, I'm not! *You* are Lianna and I am ... me!" Her shout
rang off the walls and cobbled street around her. Birds scat-

tered with a flutter and squawk at the end of the street. A couple of people stopped to stare at her. She stared back before moving on, hands shoved into the pockets of her parka and slouching against the cold.

Thoughts a babble in her mind, she wandered, aimless, past churches and through piazzas, completely unaware of anything but dodging the people she passed.

Until the grumbling in her stomach became so loud, she couldn't ignore it anymore.

She patted her pocket, relieved to feel her phone – she had a credit card tucked in the back of the case. She glanced around to find a place to eat.

Her gaze stopped and skated up the sixteen granite columns to the domed roof of the building in front of her.

The Pantheon.

"We've been here before."

"No, I haven't. Lianna di—"

Her head swam. She staggered sideways, vision shifting.

"Lianna! Lianna, come away from there!"

A woman stood a few metres away, her white *stola* flowing around her, brows pushed together in displeasure, gesturing impatiently. Four other women dressed just like her stood waiting behind her.

"Lianna. Don't let them touch you."

She pulled her arms in close, but she needn't have bothered. The crowd milled around her, but nobody was closer than two arm-spans. They kept their distance, much like for someone who carried plague.

"Do I have plague?"

"No, we're a Vestal Virgin."

Ah, Goddess. Another vision. *"Not now. Not now."*

"Yes, now."

120

She tried to push out of it, to grab onto the internal voice and separate herself from it or the memory or something; to reach for clarity where there was fog and ache and confusion.

But it was no use. The tourists that surrounded her in their jeans, warm jackets and beanies, holding their phones up to film and take selfies, dissolved, becoming people in tunics and togas, their heads bowed, hands raised, offering food and floral arrangements, dropping them at her feet as she stopped.

Their lips formed words seeking blessings, their need pressed into her. She couldn't catch her breath.

She lifted her hand to rub her aching head, the sleeve of the white gown she wore falling back to show gold armbands twining up her arm like snakes. Bracelets Clodia had put on her only this morning and told her never to take off as they were a gift from the Goddess.

But they were tight and stung her skin and ever since Clodia had put them on her, she'd felt a little strange. As if she wasn't quite herself.

Perhaps she should go inside the temple and pray. She looked up at the Pantheon of Agrippa. It wasn't Vesta's temple, but it would be cool and quiet and she could collect herself in there. And Vesta wouldn't mind if she was prayed to from another temple, even if it was Agrippa's.

"Lianna. Where are you going?"

She didn't answer, just kept moving towards the Pantheon.

"And this brings us to the Pantheon of Agrippa, or Roman Pantheon as it's mostly called."

She stumbled to a halt, looking around to see who spoke in that loud, nasal voice. They weren't speaking Latin. They were speaking ... English!

English. A language that didn't exist when she was alive. Because she wasn't alive. She was … Jules.

Jules focused in on the voice, the words as the world spun around her.

"Now simply known by most as the Pantheon, it was built in 126 AD during the reign of Hadrian. Its most notable feature is not the sixteen granite columns on its facade. Can anyone guess what it is?"

Someone bumped into her. "Sorry, love. Just tryin' to hear what our tour guide is sayin'."

Jules blinked, trying to focus on the woman in front of her – her wide smile, her brassy hair, the outrageously pink coat she wore. "Um … tour guide?"

The woman pointed at a man who was saying, "The Pantheon's most notable feature is the fact that the circular building has the exact same diameter as its height and the dome itself is bigger than the one that graces St Peter's Basilica."

"Interesting."

"It is."

She blinked, the Pantheon rising in front of her. The brassy woman and the tour group were already gone, replaced by another.

What just happened?

"You had a vision."

"Then why aren't I knocked on my arse and out for the count?"

"I have no idea. Perhaps you should figure it out."

"You think?"

A flash went off in front of her, blinding her.

She blinked rapidly, trying to clear the flare of light from her eyes. Then gasped.

It was night.

When had that happened? How long had she been lost in a vision? Hours apparently.

Shit.

How had nobody noticed? But she was glad they hadn't. She would have hated that kind of attention. Not to mention if she didn't answer, they might have called the police – or the nuthouse!

At least she didn't have to worry about that right now. What she did have to worry about was which way she needed to go to get back to the Pensione. There was no way she was missing another night of going to the Forum, no matter how upset she'd been earlier. And she wouldn't be able to go there alone. She needed the others with her to help keep her going; to look after her if she collapsed.

She spun around to figure out which direction she needed to go and came to a halt.

Bastien stood there, in his human form, wearing the jeans that made her mouth water, showing off his long, muscled legs and bottom to best effect, and a sweater that did nothing to hide the muscled breadth that lay beneath it.

Tomaso and Violetta were at his side, but she didn't have eyes for them because ...

Oh Goddess. What must he think? She swallowed hard. "I—"

"Are you okay?"

She snapped her mouth closed and breathed in sharply. He was worried about *her*? "I'm fine. I'm sorry I ran off like that. I just needed to think."

"You don't have to apologise. There's a lot to take in."

"There is."

He erased the distance between them in a few steps and took her hand in his.

Calm flowed through her. His touch. It was like home –

123

friendly, familiar, warm. Even staring into his white eyes was a balm.

Soon to be gone forever.

She forced herself to smile past the threatening tears even though he couldn't see it and answer him. "It's close to time, isn't it? Shall we go?" She took his arm and headed down the nearest street.

"Are you okay to try again? It's okay if you're not up to it—"

"No. I want to. I need to." For you.

"Then why do you sound so sad?"

She bit her lip and looked down at the cobbled street they walked down. She shrugged, not wanting to mention him leaving her again.

"Jules." He touched her cheek briefly, his mouth curling into a sad little smile. "You know you can tell me anything."

"I know. But it doesn't matter. All that matters is freeing you—"

"Us."

She nodded. "From this curse."

"You don't look so good, Jules," Tomaso said as he came up beside them, Violetta on his other side.

"I'm okay. I just had another vision."

"You did?"

"Are you okay?"

She bit her lip. "Yes. Obviously."

"But ... you're not unconscious or sick?"

She told them about what had just happened.

SIXTEEN

They all stared at her for a moment before Tomaso said, "That's amazing. Do you know how you did it?"

"I don't."

"Tell me exactly what happened and what you were doing."

She glanced over at Tomaso, taking in the fact that despite the cold, he wore one of his lovely blue suits. The man seemed to dress in nothing else.

"What he's wearing isn't important."

No it wasn't. What was important was—

Her stomach grumbled and she clutched at it, looking up sheepishly at Tomaso who was smiling at her indulgently. "Can we get something to eat first? I'm starving."

"Of course. We've got time."

"Even if we didn't, we'd get her something to eat," Bastien growled.

"Of course we would," Violetta said. "Come on, there's a pizza place on the corner there that looks a little less busy than the rest. We should be able to get something there and make it down to the Forum by midnight."

"Pizza okay?" Bastien asked her.

"Sounds perfect."

As they walked towards the hole in the wall serving pizza, she couldn't help but grimace at the thought of going down to the Forum again. A part of her didn't want to go. She didn't want to find where the curse had been created, didn't want to break the curse in three nights and see this lover of Lianna's look at her and realise she wasn't the same. Wasn't enough.

"What about Bastien?"

Bastien. She glanced up at him. Yes. She had to do it for Bastien. He needed to be freed so he could finally live his own life. And then she could get on with her life too – possibly more loveless and lonely than before, but that was a price she was willing to pay for him.

"But you'll have your magic. And Sebasti—"

She winced as the voice that was Lianna mentioned her lover's name. *"Yeah."*

Violetta ordered as they found a seat at a little wobbly table,. Minutes later she was wolfing down four slices and a big bottle of water.

When she was done, still having time to kill, they wandered through the slowly emptying streets. The cool night air caressed the heated skin of her face as they came out next to the Tyber. She wanted to stop, to stay, just stare down at the lights twinkling in its black surface.

"Do you feel like talking about what happened at the Pantheon now?" Bastien asked softly.

She nodded and started to relate how she'd found herself in front of the Pantheon and how the vision had slowly crept in. "I think I was young – I was being escorted by other Vestal Virgins. But I didn't feel well. The gold armbands Clodia had put on me that morning hurt and I just wanted to go into the cool of the Pantheon and pray to Vesta in peace and quiet."

"Gold armbands. Lianna always wore them. She couldn't take them off—" He stumbled.

"Bastien." She pulled him upright.

"Is he okay?" Violetta asked, turning to face them.

"I'm fine." He waved them on.

Jules frowned at him, but he pulled her on, asking, "Do you think it could have been the tour guide? What he said? You love learning new things."

"*It could have been because you got shoved. Or the flashes.*"

"*No. They came after. He's right. It was the information.*"

She leaned up and kissed his cheek. "You're a genius."

"Why is he a genius?" Tomaso asked.

She told him.

"That is genius. Should we give it a little trial?"

"How?"

"As we get to the concourse where it hit you hardest last time, I'll tell you something I know about the Colosseum, and we'll see what happens."

"Okay." She couldn't think of a better way to see if this information would help.

Shouts and cries started pressing into her mind as they drew closer, prickles chasing over her skin. By the time she'd stepped onto the concourse, images wavered through her mind: crowds of people rushed around her, their excitement about today's upcoming spectacle in the Flavian Amphitheatre made nausea roll in her stomach.

"Do you know how the Colosseum got its name?" Tomaso asked. She shook her head. "There was a monstrous statue the Emperor Nero commissioned of himself to show the Roman people how great he was."

She nodded. She could see the ghostly silhouette of the statue, the men who had stopped to lean on its base. Guards moved the men on, but not before she heard them agree to meet at the feet of the *Colosseo* same time next week.

"So, people started to call the monstrous statue *Colosseo*." Tomaso's voice filtered through to her. "The statue of Nero was eventually knocked down but the nickname *Colosseo* had, by that time, transferred to the amphitheatre."

"That's funny. I always hated that statue."

"It's an eyesore."

The vision faded enough for her to see three curious faces staring at her.

"It worked." Kind of. Ghost-like people rushed towards a *Colosseo* lit up by sunlight but also curiously draped in night, with lights colouring its exterior.

Bastien's ghost-like eyes glowed as he looked down at her. "I knew you'd find a way."

Always such trust. She cleared her throat. "Thanks."

"Jules? Are you okay?"

"Can we just move back? I need to catch my breath."

They bustled her back across the road, far enough away that the press of history wasn't so bad.

Tomaso clapped his hands together as she leaned against a wall, taking in deep breaths. "This is wonderful. It seems, my friends, we have a plan. Let's head home and look up interesting facts."

"Go home? But why don't we just try now?"

"That little fact only got us a few feet onto the concourse."

"But you must know more."

"I do, but not nearly enough to get you all the way to the Vestal Temple and beyond."

"But ... I don't want to lose another night."

"Better that we're fully prepared than run out of facts and lose you to a vision for another two days."

"He's right, Julianna," Violetta said softly.

Her excitement fizzled out, her shoulders sagged, exhaustion making itself fully known. "I feel like I've just put another barrier in our way."

Tomaso touched her shoulder. "On the contrary. You've just found us the way through the maze. Violetta, how about you and I head back and start searching up information? We'll meet you back at the villa."

With that, he and Violetta hurried across the road and when they were far enough away, disappeared, their magic taking them back to Tomaso's home.

Even at this distance, the magic shoved at Jules, making her stumble.

Bastien caught her, held her to him. "You okay?"

"Yep. Fine. Just disappointed."

"Don't be. This is good news. Just concentrate on that."

"He's right."

As they began to walk away from the Colosseum, the press of the past faded almost immediately. As they passed the *Area Sacra di Largo Argentina* with its community of cats, Jules had a sudden memory from her vision and stopped.

"Jules? What is it?"

"Clodia said something about an army of cats when she started her spell." She frowned over the memory. "Do you think that was a punishment she meted out to those who displeased her, like you did? Maybe some of these cats are actually the ancestors of people she cursed."

He shook his head, mouth cocked a little on one side. "No. I think that punishment is unique to me."

"Maybe I should come back and check these are all actually cats after I get my powers back."

"Yes, *we* should." He turned, reaching out to cup her face, a deep frown furrowing his brows.

"Bas? What is it?"

He cleared his throat. "What you said before, about me leaving you. You don't have to worry about that. I promise."

She wrapped her cold fingers around his warm wrists, trying to steady herself, blink away the tears. "Don't make promises you might not want to keep."

"It might be you who doesn't want me with you."

She chuckled, a hoarse, broken sound. "Never going to happen." She expected the voice to say something, but it stayed curiously silent.

Their breaths mingled visibly in the air between them for long moments, then he leaned down and pressed his lips to her forehead, their warmth lingering as he pulled away.

She sucked in a breath and closed her eyes, his scent all around her. Oh Gods. It hurt too much to think of him going away, but despite what he said, she wouldn't hold him to her. He deserved his freedom.

He smiled as he tucked her arm in his again. "Tell me more about the Rome you see."

Her voice was hoarse by the time they made it back to the villa. Once inside, Violetta insisted she go upstairs to rest and leave them to search out the reams of information they'd need for their try tomorrow night.

"But don't you need my help?"

"It's best if we tell you things you might not have heard."

"Bas can stay," Tomaso said. "He and Violetta will know best what you'll find interesting."

Bastien made a sorry face, but before he went to join Tomaso said, "I'll be up before I change."

"Okay."

She headed upstairs, frustratingly aware she only had two more nights to get everything right. The thought of breaking their curse and freeing Bastien should make her happy – instead, she struggled not to break into tears.

CHAPTER
SEVENTEEN

"Are you ready?" Bastien asked.

"Sure."

"You don't sound very confident."

"Shut up."

The last twenty-four hours had been an unendurable wait until it was time to try again. But finally it was here. And she had to succeed.

The clocks struck twelve in the city around them, signifying the change from the eleventh to the twelfth. She came to a stop opposite the Colosseum, clutched Bastien's arm even though he was still recovering from his change just over an hour ago – so much later than the day before.

Screams and the vibration of pain from the ruins opposite thrummed through her.

Tomaso lifted the folder he carried. "Shall I read this out to you? Or do you want Violetta to do it?"

She wished Bastien could do it. But she couldn't ask him – even if he wasn't blind – because he was still too weak. "You do it," she said to Tomaso.

"Everyone okay with that?"

"Absolutely," Bastien said, his voice husky and threaded with pain.

"Let's do this," Violetta said. "Before the security guards come back this way."

Jules nodded. She swallowed hard then whispered to Bastien, "Don't let go, okay?"

"I won't." His hand slipped down to hers, squeezed.

Together they stepped off the curb.

At least if she succeeded, she'd be happy to set Bastien free to pursue his own life. And she'd have the second-hand love of her lover to—

She winced as the curse stabbed her in the chest.

"Jules?"

"Fine," she said, straightening up, rubbing her knuckles against her chest surreptitiously. "I just thought something I obviously shouldn't."

"Yeah, I'm having problems with that too." His voice was strained. He looked worse than he had when he'd come downstairs after his change.

"Do you need to sit down?"

"No. I just need to stop thinking about what we're here for."

He leaned on her more heavily as they walked forward. She held on tight, struggling to keep herself upright in the face of what the curse threw at her.

"I think we need to start now," Bastien said as they drew even with the others at the edge of the concourse.

"You okay?"

Bastien nodded stiffly. "Just the curse making itself known."

"And what about you?" Tomaso asked Jules.

She rubbed the side of her head. "It's loud in here and my vision is starting to fog. I can see ghostly people over there."

"Right then, let's get started before it becomes too bad. Try to empty your mind and open it up only to the flow of information I read."

She nodded and took a step forward as Tomaso began to speak about the Colosseum and surrounds.

Shouts. Screams. Jeers. Cheers. They rose to greet her, louder and louder with every step. Pressing in.

"Concentrate on what Tomaso is saying," Bastien whispered – or maybe he shouted. It was hard to know over the noise wrapping around her.

"On our left, you will see the remains of the ancient fountain the gladiators used to wash in after a match. Unfortunately, there is little left of this remarkable piece of Roman ingenuity due to the fact Mussolini drove over it in a tank because it was in the way of his parade!"

"A tank. Wish we'd seen that."

"It would have been awful. How could he destroy something with so many stories?"

She could see the fountain, ghostly gladiators washing themselves in the late afternoon sun, slapping each other's backs. A woman ran up and gave one of them a hug.

"Aww."

"He's all sweaty."

"You're just jealous because you've never hugged a man like that."

"I have. I've had sex!"

"Once. And you never held him like that. Nor he you."

It was true. That time had been with a friend at uni who had agreed to help her pop her cherry. It had been nice - and awkward - but had none of the emotions that the ghostly couple were happy to show each other in public. Only Leanna fully knew how that kind of intimacy felt. But that had been thousands of years ago.

It wasn't fair. It was—

Ah Hells. She *was* jealous.

But it had been so long since anyone had touched her with kindness or affection, except Esta – and her cousin didn't count.

Lianna longed to be touched. Ached for it.

Wait. What? No. You're Jules. Not Lianna. Don't give in to it. Listen to Tomaso. Listen to ...

A sharp pain in her shoulder. "Ouch." She reached up to rub it, turning to see who had thrown whatever it was, ready to give them a serve. The words died as her gaze met the most beautiful peridot-coloured eyes. No, they were white eyes. Now peridot. Strange. But not strange.

The owner of the eyes strode closer until he stood so close he could touch her. Then he smiled down at her, his fingers brushing over the sting on her shoulder. It disappeared. *"Scuzi, bella,"* he murmured. "This was not meant for you."

Oh. His voice. It was like a caress. As she looked up at him, the world spun.

"Lianna." She blinked. Looked down at the young girl before her, dressed all in white. "I didn't think we were supposed to talk to strange men. Won't Clodia be angry?"

"Not if we don't tell her," she whispered, touching little Esta's nose through the veil, delighting in the smile that lit the young girl's face. She let her young companion drag her away, but she couldn't help turning to look back at the man, his broad shoulders and tapered-in waist limned by the sun. He glowed.

He watched her with his unusual eyes, which oscillated

from peridot to white. His features were strangely unclear, but she knew he was handsome, with a devilish smile. And the aura of power emanating from him – she'd never come across anything like it.

Who was he? She longed to find out. Maybe she would. It couldn't hurt to discover his name.

She held up her hand, indicating she wanted him to wait there – that she'd be back in one hour. Would he understand?

He nodded.

Excitement tingled through every pore as she followed Esta through the crowds to the temple. One hour. Then she would return to the fountain and assuage her curiosity ...

"Jules. Jules? Can you hear me? She's coming around, I think."

Jules opened her eyes and looked up to see three faces looking down at her. Their expressions were hidden in the night's shadows, their heads haloed by the lights of the Colosseum behind them. "Shit." She forced herself to sit and clutched her head, groaning. "I passed out, didn't I?"

"Yes."

She rubbed the heels of her hands into her aching head as she stared at the hulk of the Colosseum opposite them. "How far did I get?"

"Further than before," Violetta said, a strange smile pulling at her lips. It wasn't very reassuring.

"How far?"

"Almost to the entrance of the Forum."

She groaned. Still not close enough. "What time is it?" Bastien was still in human form, so at least there was that. She really didn't think she was going to be able to do this without the feel of his hand in hers.

"It's twelve-thirty."

Bastien changed at two last night, so given the regression, he had until one, maybe one-thirty. "Okay. Let's go again."

The world swayed as she went to stand. She sat down with a plop.

"Take it easy," Violetta muttered.

"I can't take it easy. We don't have time."

"You won't be able to try again if you can't even stand without falling over."

"She's right."

"I don't have time to baby myself. Look at Bastien."

"He looks terrible."

The curse was really punishing him tonight – or was he nearing his change?

"It's time to be his hero. I need to put on my Wonder-Woman-big-girl-pants."

"Did we pack any of those?"

She huffed out a laugh.

"Jules?"

"I'm good." She took a few steadying breaths then pushed to her knees. The world swayed a little, but not as bad as before. After a few more deep breaths, she made it to her feet.

"You good?" Bastien said.

She took his outstretched hand. "I'm good. Let's go again." She glanced over at Tomaso. "Could you stand closer and talk louder? I could barely hear you over the ghosts in my head."

"I didn't want to be too loud in case there are guards around. My spell on the equipment and some of the surrounds won't cover the noise we make."

"I'll take care of any guards if they come running," Violetta said.

"But Jules won't be able to take the magic you use."

"I'll move as far away as I can without losing sight of you. That should help mitigate the problem."

"Do it." Jules was happy to put up with more pain if it kept everyone else safe from being caught.

They let Violetta go ahead then moved off.

CHAPTER
EIGHTEEN

Voices and screams rushed at her as she continued along the concourse past the Colleseum but Tomaso stood right beside her this time, talking loudly. She still had to concentrate on his words – the noise of the past was louder this time – but she heard enough to keep the visions at bay.

As they drew closer to the Forum, the visions pressed in on her, closer, louder. The buzz chasing over her skin turned into a prickling pain. The urge to stop, to turn around and run back the way she'd come, or submit to the darkness creeping at the edges of her vision, increased with every step, every harsh breath, but she couldn't give in. Couldn't give up. This was something she had to do if she wanted Bastien to go free. If anyone deserved more than her best effort, it was her best friend.

"That's it, Jules," Bastien said, his breath hot on her ear, his voice barely audible above the noise around her. She clung to his hand as the bits of history Tomaso related conjured up images of what it must have been like in ancient times – visions she remained in control of. The further they went, though, the harder it got. Her head was full, so full, it felt too heavy on her neck. So heavy it might just fall off.

"*Off with his head.*"

"*They didn't do that here. That's more a French Revolution thing.*"

"*Or a Queen of Hearts thing. Off with his head. Off with hishhead. Offwishhishead!*"

She giggled.

"Why is she giggling?"

"I don't know."

"Jules! Concentrate."

She took in a deep breath and shook her head. "I'm good. More. Louder."

Tomaso started shouting information, his lips almost up against her ear. The words helped to build a wall against the visions.

"Ahead is the rostra where speeches were made to the Roman people."

Her vision shimmered and she blinked rapidly to clear it. It was difficult to see what she knew was before her – the ruins. All she could see was a man standing on a rostra, temples and other marble buildings shining in the sun behind him. "Many a senator stood on the rostra here to talk to the people of *Roma*, but you could also find any man with a voice and a thought and the will to speak having their say. It's thought that Julius Caesar himself ..."

His voice disappeared into the angry shouts of the crowd throwing things at the man on the rostra, his gestures and expression impassioned, pleading with them to listen.

"Lianna. Where have you got to? I need you in the temple now."

Clodia, her white gown flowing around her, her anger evident even with the veil shrouding her face, moved through the crowd nearby, obviously searching for her but not seeing her. The golden bands on Lianna's arms tightened, but she held out against their insistence – she'd already done her service for today and was wrung out. She needed more time—

A hand gripped her arm and pulled her around a corner, out of sight of her High Priestess. She looked up.

His face was hidden in shadow, but she knew him, his touch, the tall, muscled strength of him glowing with power, his beautiful eyes. "Sebastio."

"Meet me at ten at our usual place."

She nodded, breathless as he lifted her veil to kiss her, lips lingering, hands cupping her face in that way she adored. "I love you," he said, before letting go and disappearing into the crowd.

She hadn't returned his words of love. She would make certain he heard them tonight.

Tonight.

She pulled her veil over her face to hide her smile and moved out quickly into the crowd towards Clodia. Thankfully, the High Priestess hadn't seen her meeting with Sebastio, or her anger would be far greater than the annoyance she showed as Lianna drew near.

Lianna hated the need to keep their love a secret, but she would not be free from her service to Vesta for another few months, so she had no choice.

She had no idea how she would keep the secret for that long, but she would. It was imperative. She couldn't give him up, so hiding and secrecy were the only options.

"Jules. Listen to Tomaso. Don't let anything else get between you and his voice."

She gasped for breath as the voice she knew so well echoed through her mind.

Bastien.

"He's talking to you. Not me."

"I can't feel him."

"Hold more tightly. He's there."

"It would be easier if you kept your memories out of my head."

"I can't. They're your memories too."

She didn't have the energy to argue, so gripped Bastien's arm more tightly, leaning into him. He stumbled, too weak to hold his own weight, let alone hers. She loosened her grip. She could see Violetta standing on some stones at the end of the path, something about her stance suggesting worry and fury. She had to get this done. "How far?"

"Not far," he said. He stumbled again. Goddess, what was this doing to him? She let go of him.

Ghostly figures crowded around her. Darkness edged her vision, Tomaso's voice a bare whisper in the distance despite feeling his breath flutter her hair as he spoke right next to her ear. Her head rang with the cries of the ancient crowd surrounding her in the midday sun. Except, it wasn't day. It was the middle of the night. And the buildings around her were no longer shining monoliths to Rome's glory, but rubble and dust.

She gasped, trying to catch her breath. Her heart pounded and her knees trembled. She stumbled, caught herself, kept going.

"Jules? Jules, are you okay?"

She nodded.

"I'm so sorry. I can't touch you to help you. Even

holding back my power I could still send you spiralling into a vision or hurt you if I did. Can you keep going?"

"More ... info."

Her head swam as they made their way down into the ruins, the pain increasing. Her companions were mere shadows around her, their presence, their words, helping, but every step was a nightmare as her vision schismed between the past and the present. But she had to do this. Had to.

They passed the Temple of the Priestesses of Vesta.

"Home. Where I'm keeper of the holy flame."

"No. That was me. You're Jules Stevens, Coven librarian."

"Failed witch."

"Don't call yourself that."

The repartee with the Lianna-presence gave her something else to cling to. Breath sawed in and out of her chest, the pain intensifying with every step she took.

Something warm slung around her shoulders, squeezed. "Jules. You're doing it."

Bas.

One step. Another.

And another.

For Bastien.

Her lungs squeezed. Tears streamed from her eyes and she could barely see – not the ruins, not the images of ancient temples and buildings she knew so well.

Oh Goddess. It wasn't going to be enough. She was fading, falling, neither here nor there. Not Jules or Julianna or Lianna. She was nothing but pain and a screaming rage that filled her ears and took everything from her.

"The magic of the pentacle. Look, there it is! She's found it."

"I knew she would."

"Tomaso, help me get Jules up. She can't touch it any longer. She's already bleeding."

"My power."

"Pull it right back and touch nothing but her jacket. The combination of your jacket and hers should act as enough of a shield to protect her from anything you can't keep from slipping out."

She was lifted, relief shuddering through her as the pain lessened, but the world still spun around her, nausea a sickening roil in her stomach. She was put down to lean against a large stone. Bastien's arm went around her again, his lips near her ear. "You did it. You did it."

"By Eros's grace. It's glowing faintly. Can you see it? How could we have not seen this before, Violetta?"

Jules barely had a moment to register the joy of her success before Bastien's cry of pain lit the night. His entire body tensed then jerked violently, the arm around her shoulders a crushing weight, bearing them both to the ground.

"Bastien!"

"Jules, run. Get away."

But she couldn't. Couldn't let go of him. The magic of his change, the darkness and pain, sucked her into their madness and everything was gone.

CHAPTER
NINETEEN

J ules didn't wake until the day was almost over. It had been an agony just to sit there and will her to wake in time, but it was even more of an agony to watch her once she finally did.

She barely touched the meal Violetta brought her, instead sitting on the window seat to stare out the window at the gathering shadows of night, flinching at every strike of the city's bells as the hours passed.

The slump of her shoulders and the stiff line of her back told him all he needed to know about how she felt. Tension sang from her, almost as loud as the *Carnevale* celebrations lifting from the streets and plaza below.

Bastien wished he could tell her everything was going to be okay, that despite her thinking she was weak, she was the strongest person he knew. He wished, like Violetta had said, that he could do more to show her how he felt about her, was trying to will that knowledge from himself and into her with everything in him. But it wasn't good enough. He couldn't truly show her through word or gesture – which he would despite the pain, despite her disliking intensely when he was in pain – but he couldn't say any of it.

He was still a cat. All he could do was sit on the bed brushed up against her purring, and watch her.

Damn his changes. It was bad enough it took so much out of him, but that it had almost taken down Jules ... Even though Tamuel had grabbed him and magicked him away, it hadn't been fast enough – or far enough away. There hadn't been time. The magic of his change had already begun to cut into Jules – there had been so much blood – so rather than pull Bastien away, Tamuel had just grabbed him and gone.

The scream that had followed them – Hells. He thought he'd killed her. Somehow though, she hadn't been too badly hurt. Lots of bruises and shallow cuts, the worse one on her forehead from when Tamuel's translocation magic had hit her. Thankfully it hadn't needed stitches. All that magic so close had drained her though, far too much. She looked almost as bad as he felt.

She turned back now to smile at him, face drawn, the bandage on her brow just under her hairline only a little paler than her face.

She touched it. "Please, Bastien. Don't blame yourself. It's not your fault."

He wished he could tell her it wasn't her fault either. It would have to wait until he changed tonight.

But his change, when it came just before eleven, was brutal.

Afterwards, he needed Tamuel's help to shower and change and get downstairs, helping him to sit in the chair at the little table outside opposite Jules. Her aura was slow and a little muddy, but not as bad as it was when she woke. Still, she wasn't herself.

As he ate, Tamuel announced they wouldn't try for the Forum again tonight. "We have discovered what works to get you into place, Jules, but need to find more information to grab your attention and help keep you in the now."

"I think it's good idea," Violetta said before either he or Jules could protest. "Besides, I think it best if you both preserve your energy. You're going to need it tomorrow night."

"I'm fine. If Jules wants to go down and try again, I'll be ready." He had to be.

"No, you're not. You look like shit."

"Stop trying to baby me," he snapped to Tamuel with mind-speech. *"I won't let this curse stop me from helping Jules break it."*

Tamuel placed his hand on Bastien's shoulder, the buzz of power giving Bastien a little boost of energy with that strange non-magic-magic he was able to tap into now and then. *"Of course not. But while I can help you with a little boost of power, I cannot do so for Jules. She's exhausted. She must rest. Surely you can see that in her aura? But she will go down there again if you say you're okay. We can't let her do that. Not if we want her to be as strong as possible tomorrow night. Given what's been happening to you, losing so many hours in your human form, this might be our last chance."*

Bastien fell silent, then said, "Actually, I do feel terrible. Resting up tonight and researching more information sounds good." He picked up a chop and tore into it.

Jules slipped onto the bench beside him. "Is it really that bad?"

"This is helping," he said, waving the chop bone, wishing once again that he could see her. Truly see her while in this form.

She cleared her throat but said nothing.

147

"Eat up, Bastien," Violetta said briskly. "Then Jules best head upstairs and get a good night's rest. Bastien, you can do some research for a few hours, but then you need to rest too."

"That's my cue to go then," Tamuel said, standing and grabbing his coat.

"Go where?"

Tamuel's aura twinkled. "Our success last night helped me pin down where the HeartsBlood Gem is. And it's probably better I get it tonight than risk waiting until tomorrow. I'd also like to do some prep on the area to make certain everything is as ready as it can be for tomorrow night. Rest up, Bastien. You too, Jules. I'll see you all tomorrow."

Jules, at Violetta's urging, left Bastien to finish his three plates of food in silence and think over everything that had happened so far. Violetta disappeared as well after saying she was off to the Roman Coven to find some more information that covered the magical history of the area around the Forum.

Bastien finished eating and then spent an hour doing research and writing down some notes for Tamuel. But after an hour, he struggled to focus, his gaze returning more often to the stairs. He still had two hours as a human. He didn't want to spend it alone researching or sleeping. He wanted to talk to Jules now. Needed to talk to her, to touch her one more time as a human, to try to show her through touch if not through word that he loved her. It was virtually all he could do for her before whatever happened tomorrow night.

He made his way upstairs to her room and halted outside.

There was no sound. He pushed the door open.

Soft sounds of her sleeping reached him – she really was

exhausted. Even though he ached to talk to her, to hold her one more time before everything changed, he backed out of the room, closing the door quietly behind him.

JULES AWOKE MID-MORNING, feeling far more refreshed than she had in days. She blinked into the bright sunlight streaming into the room, then sat upright with a gasp.

She'd missed talking to Bastien last night before he changed back into a cat.

She spun. He was on the bed, curled up and fast asleep – he must have come in after his change. She ran her hand over his soft head and down his body – so thin – but he didn't wake, so she left him alone and went downstairs to prepare food for him.

When he finally padded into the kitchen an hour later, she turned with a bright smile on her face. "You're awake. I've made you all your favourites." She gestured to the table. He gave a grateful meow, leaped up and began to eat.

She continued to cut up more ham. She'd never felt the need to fill the silence with him, but now, suddenly, she couldn't stand it. "So, Valentine's Eve tonight. Big one, hey? Maybe by Valentine's Day, we'll both get our happy ever afters." Her face crumpled.

Oh Goddess. What did I say that for?

She tried to pull it together, but it didn't work. Already, she felt the loss of her best friend in all the world – the one person who wasn't family who liked her for her. Maybe even loved her for her.

Pain spiked through her head at the thought, but she hid her wince, spinning away from Bastien's curious gaze.

"I need to clean my teeth," she said and rushed out, sprinting up the stairs and into their room.

She went into the bathroom and only then realised she still had the big knife in her hand she'd used to cut the ham. She put it down with a shaky hand and tried to breathe, tried not to vomit, tried to just keep her shit together. But it was so hard.

"Don't you want to help him?"

"Of course I do. But I'm going to miss him." She rubbed her chest. *"I just wish Bastien could be my forever love, my soulmate — Agh!"*

She pushed the base of her palm into her eye where pain stabbed. "Bloody, stupid, idiot, bastard, fuckity-shit curse," she said, smacking her other fist against the bathroom counter, the sting on her knuckles bright and an almost welcome relief against the throb in her head and the heavy sensation of claustrophobia squeezing around her heart.

"If Clodia wasn't already dead—"

She looked down at the knife she'd picked up.

"I've long wanted to stab that ancient bitch-witch in her cold dead heart."

Wow, she never realised she had such violent urges. Or were they Lianna's urges? It was hard to know. How could she trust how she felt about her lo— No. She wasn't going to think about him.

"Meow?"

She swung around to see Bastien sitting in the doorway, eyes full of her pain. "Don't," she said to him, rushing past to stare out the window. She couldn't face him now – not with this raw, empty hole in her heart. It was like he'd already left her and she was left with ... nothing but memories.

But of course, Bastien being Bastien leaped up on the windowsill, rearing up to put his paws on her shoulders and look in her eyes.

"Bastien," she said, unable to stop from meeting his unblinking gaze. Such beautiful peridot eyes.

Peridot eyes like Seba—!

Pain exploded behind her eyes, her vision fracturing, split between Bastien's peridot-coloured cat-eyes and a pair of long-lashed almond-shaped eyes, the flashes of gold and emerald in the depths sparking with heat and an eternal passion she dreamed of every night since ... since ... he'd been taken from her by Clodia and cursed.

"Bastien," she whispered. "Bas ... tien. Bas ... Bas." Darkness flew towards her and she was falling, falling ...

So lonely. She knew there was only a month to go, but she needed Bas now.

Power flared around her and he appeared as if he'd heard her need.

He always came when she needed him.

"Sebastio. My Bas." She held her arms out.

"Lianna," he said, his deep voice a caress. "My love."

"I need you."

"Come." He wrapped his muscled arms around her, holding her close to his warmth, then transported them away. They landed softly in the bed he'd made for them in a little cottage in the forest. Their clothes were already gone – all except her golden armbands that never came off. His magic tingled against her skin, caressing, making her gasp.

He rolled over her, bare skin sliding against bare skin as his lips took hers. Passion that had simmered for the days she'd been without him flared to vibrant, all-consuming life. Their tongues tangled, his breath becoming hers. His taste – oranges and spice – filled her mouth. She moaned deep in her throat. It was her favourite flavour, essence of Bas. As was his scent – spicy and citrus with a bit of something deeper, like fresh-cut wood.

Her hands dug into the silkiness of his thick black hair as his mouth left hers to explore her neck and shoulders. "I love you," he said between nips and licks and suckles.

"I love you too," she gasped.

His hands were on her breasts, then his lips were there. She cried out as he sucked a nipple into his mouth, his free hand diving into the curls at the juncture of her thighs, stroking in time to his licks and sucks in that way that drove all thought out of her head and lit lightning sparks behind her eyelids.

"Look at me, Lianna. Look at me."

She opened her eyes and met his gaze. Such fire in the beautiful green-gold depths. It made her gasp and shiver as he drove a finger inside her, then another, his thumb playing her pleasure like a finely tuned harp. He kept his gaze locked on hers as he pushed her into orgasm then over the edge once, twice, three times, ignoring her begs and pleas to come inside her.

But then finally – finally – he was there, the thickness of his erection pushing into the slick heat of her, filling her in one quick glide. She moaned, her fingers digging into his hip and back as he seated himself deep inside her and began to move.

Slow – oh so torturously slow. He loved to tease her with his control. But she knew some tricks herself.

She ground herself against him, fingers moving over his deliciously pouty bottom, up his back and into his hair. She pulled his head down for a long, gloriously wet kiss before kissing a path down his strong neck to the glory of his shoulders. Then she bit down on the place between neck and shoulder where his pulse beat fast and strong.

"Witch," he groaned, then pumped faster, deeper, harder, just as she needed him to.

"God," she shouted as her muscles clenched, riding his rhythm.

"Demi-God," he said, full lips quirked in that bewitching smile she so loved.

"*My* demi-God," she said, before capturing his mouth for another long, lingering kiss.

He reared back. Gazes clashed, held as their hands gripped. Stars sparked as the wave broke over her, through her, their cries of shared passion joining in the night, a magical note of joy.

CHAPTER
TWENTY

Lianna came to, wrapped in his arms, legs tangled, her face pressed against the warm strength of his chest, his breath brushing over her crown. She looked up. Their gazes met. He smiled and pressed a kiss to her forehead, then one to her lips.

She settled back against him and revelled in the sensation of being here with him.

Home. Love. Fulfilment. She'd never thought to have any of these things and yet Bas gave them to her every time they were together and promised a lifetime more when she was finally free.

There was a little slither of guilt that she'd broken her vows – but there had been no stopping this once they'd met. One look and they were lost in each other. It didn't even have anything to do with the cupid's arrow he'd loosed at the woman behind her but had accidentally hit her instead. She'd never needed Bas' assurances that he hadn't 'done an Eros and Psyche', as he called it. That bolt meant for another had never worked on her. All it had done was made her turn and see him. The fact they were soul-mates had taken care of the rest.

Still, it made her a little nervous. The timing was terrible – she had only a few months left of her service. She should have held back, but she couldn't. Neither of them could. And now there were only a few months to go until she could be with Bas openly and honestly.

A few more months to be in Clodia's control. Until she could remove these horrid golden armbands that ceded her powers to Clodia while she was in the service of Vesta. She touched one now, cold where it should be warm.

Clodia said their Goddess had given Lianna the powers of a High Priestess by mistake, that she was too weak-hearted and not intelligent enough to hold her own among the cut-throat Senate and High Priesthood of *Roma*.

"I'm doing you a favour," she'd told Lianna time and time again as she'd sapped her of her power to use in the Goddess's name, to increase the hold she held over the Senate and the people in her machinations to make the Coven of the Temple Vesta a true power. To stay in power herself.

She should have stepped down years ago, but Lianna's power enabled her to keep her youth and position – and if Lianna had to put up with a bit of pain and Clodia's temper tantrums about power being given to the undeserving, she was happy to do it if it meant she never had to become like Clodia.

Power corrupted. She almost wished at times she could get rid of hers. If she had, then she wouldn't be in this position now. She would never have been a Vestal Virgin and would have been able to be with Bas free and clear right from the moment they met.

"Not long now," he murmured, speaking her thoughts out loud as he often did.

"I just hope she doesn't turn her eye to Esta."

He nuzzled her neck, his erection brushing against her side. "She won't. Esta isn't powerful enough to tempt her. She'll be looking for another Goddess-touched witch like you to use. Esta will be safe. And you will soon be free and have full control over your powers. I can't wait to teach you a thing or two."

"Really," she said, rolling over him and taking him inside her again. "Perhaps you could teach me now."

"Perhaps I could."

After their passion was spent for a second time, she snuggled down, cuddling Bas's head to her chest, rubbing her cheek against him.

He yawned. His hand brushed over her stomach, then froze.

"Lianna." He bolted upright, lines of confusion furrowing his brow. He moved his hand over her stomach again as his eyes met hers. "Lianna. There is life growing in your womb."

"What? No. That's impossible." She sat up, shaking her head. "I've spelled precautions. I should not be able to fall pregnant until I release them." The dregs of power she had access to were strong enough for that.

He ran his hand over her stomach again. "I'm not wrong. I can feel him. Our son. Growing even now."

She grasped at her stomach. "Impossible." But it wasn't. She felt what he felt. The spark of life inside her growing where it shouldn't be able to grow.

How was this possible? She closed her eyes and checked her binding spell.

It had a break in it. A black thread of Clodia's control had snaked out from the armband and sliced through the binding. She was no longer protected against the seed of a demi-God.

"No. No." This was proof she'd broken her vow.

"It will be okay. It is just taken. You will be free before anyone knows."

"But the babe ... it will grow faster than usual because of who you are. I will show in a few weeks."

"You will come to term in seven months rather than nine, true. But that is not a worry in itself. Babes are born before their time often enough for nobody to pay much attention to the exact length of your pregnancy. And for the next few months I'll help to keep the babe hidden. It will be fine. All will be well. Soon you will be free and then we will be together in full – you me and our son."

She wanted to cling to his words, to hold onto them and never let go, but realisation hit her, making her feel sick. "You don't understand. She won't let me go. She never intended to. She did this on purpose. She'll use this to bind my power to her forever."

He frowned down at her. "What? What are you talking about?"

She explained about the thread of power from the armband that had done away with her precautions against falling pregnant. "I don't know how, but she knows about us. She did this purposefully. She wants me to be found guilty of treason so she can take my power in full and call it hers."

"I won't let that happen.

"How? She'll sense your interference. And she's too clever not to have thought of every single plan we might

157

make to get out of this. Oh Goddess. If she accuses me of treason and I am buried alive, she'll be able to syphon off my power and I won't be able to stop her. She made certain of that."

She touched one of the gold bands on her arms then clutched her stomach. "This is the proof she needs so that she can do it with nobody able to stop her. To take my powers for her own. I knew she seemed too accepting about my time under her power coming to an end. She meant for this to happen." Her gaze slammed into his. "Oh, Bas. Is she the reason we fell in love? Your bolts never miss their target – so why did you hit me?"

He grasped her hands. "I don't know. But it didn't work, so even if she was involved, it has no bearing on this. You are my soulmate."

"That is just a lucky coincidence. I know she did this. She meant for that bolt to hit me so I would fall in love with you. She didn't need for us to be soulmates." Her stomach rolled and she swallowed down bile, trying not to show how truly frightened and panicked she was.

"I know she did this. She made it so I would break my vows and now she's going to use it for her own gain." Goddess – if she could do this to one of her own Coven, then what would she do to anyone else who got in her way?

Tears streaming down her face, she pushed away from him. "You have to go. Save yourself."

"I will never leave you and our child."

"But you must." She shoved at him, trying to get him to leave their bed. "It is our only chance. I fear she will soon discover this pregnancy through whatever magic she has spelled these armbands with. She will strike quickly. I need you to be safe from her machinations. I need you to make sure our child is safe."

"I'm a demi-God. What can she do to me?"

"This."

Lianna swung around at the sound of Clodia's voice behind her. The High Priestess stood in the doorway, eyes gleaming in the red glow of the gem she wore around her neck. "No!"

Bas made a choking sound. She turned to see him frozen in place, mouth open, eyes popping like he was choking.

"Stop. Stop! What are you doing?" She scrambled off the bed, legs tangling in the sheets, and landed at Clodia's feet to look up into eyes of madness. "Please. Please stop this. I'll do anything you want. Just don't hurt him. Don't hurt our child."

Clodia cackled. "I have you now." She gripped Lianna's arm, fingers pinching, and hauled her to her feet. "You thought you could leave me and have it all – a man, a child, a happy life and the power that was meant to be mine too?" She leaned in, her spittle sizzling on Lianna's cheeks as she spoke. "You will never have your true love and perfect life. They, like your powers, belong to me now."

She put her hand over Lianna's stomach. "He's already quickening." Lianna looked down to see her stomach expand, the child inside her growing ten times faster than even the son of a demi-God would because of the powers that lived in his cells.

"Stop it!" she screamed at Clodia. "Stop this. Don't touch my babe. Leave him alone!"

Clodia cackled. "Leave him alone? Why would I do that when this is what I've been waiting for? The child of a demi-God and a Goddess-touched witch. That power will make him even more valuable to me than you and he'll be in my grasp so very soon."

"No! No!" she cried, trying to engage her powers, to save herself, Sebastio, their child, but Clodia lifted the glowing red gem, its red-heart pulsing with a sickening throb, and she was falling, falling ...

... "Wake up. Wake up, you silly bitch."

CHAPTER
TWENTY-ONE

Jules' cheek stung as a slap sounded in the air. She blinked, pulling herself up and out of the vision.

"Wake up. Faster." Another slap.

Head ringing, she raised her arms in protection, peering through them to see who was hitting her. "Grandmama?" Violetta had slapped her?

"I am not your grandmama. By the Goddess, are you too stupid to see?" She lifted her hands as if to showcase herself. Her perfect bob was a crackling halo around her head, and her features kept flickering between her own and someone else's.

"Clodia."

"Are you sure?"

"Yes."

"Clodia?"

The ancient witch wearing Violetta's face smiled viciously. "Yes. Your grandmama came snooping around my temple the night she arrived in *Roma*. So eager was she to help break my curse, to try to gain back more of Esta's memories, that she stupidly came to the temple ruins at the

161

witching hour and called on the spirits. The moment she did, she opened herself to me and I slipped in. I've been with her, controlling her, since before you arrived."

Jules pushed herself upright from where she'd slumped on the floor. The room swayed around her as she gasped, "How were you still there?"

Clodia chuckled, low and raspy. "I've been haunting the place, knowing you'd be back one day to break my curse. It took far longer for you to grow some gumption to get you here, but finally, here you are."

"But why take Violetta?"

She sniffed. "She was easy pickings. I've been pretty convincing, don't you think?" She patted her hair. "Even the cupid didn't know it was me." Her smirk made icy fingers crawl up Jules's spine.

"What cupid?"

Clodia snorted out a laugh. "Your son, of course. Tamuel. Sorry, I mean Tomaso." She chuckled. "Clever cupid escaped me all those years ago somehow even though he was but a new-born; and he almost escaped me now. I would never have guessed who he was if he hadn't used his magic to whisk Sebastio away from the Forum two nights ago. He didn't even think to mask his magical scent. So like his father."

"His father?"

"Your lover, of course. Sebastio. Bas. Bastien." She pointed at him – he stood frozen on the bed, back arched, fur ruffled, mid-hiss. "He's not the servant you thought he was. There was never any servant – that was just a false memory planted to make it so you never remembered who he was. Although, given all the visions you've been having, I thought maybe you had guessed. I guess my curse is not as weakened as I thought."

"Weakened?" Was she crazy? "It's stronger than ever."

Clodia snorted. "You're stupider than Lianna ever was. And more gullible. The curse hasn't been getting stronger. If it had, you would never have seen the things you've seen in your dreams and visions and you wouldn't have been able to speak to Bastien, let alone be friends with him. Violetta had started to suspect how weak the curse was becoming, but thankfully I got to her before she could mention anything. And then it was a simple matter to make you all think it was strengthening with the help of all this lovely magic she has access to. Do you know how delicious it's been, using your beloved grandmama's magic against you?" Her smile was horrible – Violetta's face moving in a way it never had before. "It was so much fun to make things harder for you. You always had it too easy."

"Easy? You think I've had it easy?"

"In comparison to me? Yes! I always had to work so hard for everything I got, but you! You just got it all handed to you at birth. And why? For no good reason I could ever figure out. I'm stronger and smarter than you would ever be. I should have been the one to get Vesta's power." She struck herself in the chest. "It should have been me." Her vicious expression morphed into something close to pure evil as she leaned forward and whispered. "And now I am about to get my due, finally."

Jules pulled back as far as she could. "You won't win. I'm going to break the curse."

"Goodie." She clapped her hands, cackling.

"What?" What did she mean 'good'.

"Oh, the look on your face. You think I was trying to stop you from breaking the curse? On the contrary, I've been waiting here since my death, unable to take my rightful power or place among the Gods." She leaned closer again, the ghostly eyes behind Violetta's manic. "I will break the curse at midnight on this Valentine Eve so that your magic is free once more. And then and only then I can slowly drain you of power as I meant to do 2,000 years ago, and you will be unable to stop it."

"Tomaso will stop you."

Clodia's shriek of laughter rang around the room, making Jules' head throb more. "Tamuel has already been bound into the pentacle."

"What? But he went to get the HeartsBlood Gem."

"And he never came back."

"Yes. You were right about where it was. After your power failed to come to me, powering my curse in a way I never intended when it buried itself deep inside you, I couldn't make the HeartsBlood Gem move from your burial place. I had to leave it there, in its own grave at the heart of the pentacle. Tamuel was so thrilled to find it, he didn't even question why I was there as he freed it – something he could do only because he is your son despite the fact it is magic only meant for women of power to use. But once he'd freed it, it was easy enough to take it and use it, as I did against Sebastio, binding him to the pentacle as I did the night of his birth and hiding his presence from everyone until I am ready to cast my spell."

"You're a monster."

"No. I'm a Goddess in the making. Now, for your instructions for tonight's events."

Jules struggled up from the floor, limbs heavy and uncooperative. "You can't make me do anything – if you could, you already would have."

"True. Like that night centuries ago, you had to agree to be there of your own free will. And like that night, I will use your love against you. When I threatened to abort your unborn babe, you agreed so easily." She flung out her hands. There was a pop of noise and a rush of wind and suddenly Bastien lay in her arms.

'No!' Jules took a stumbling step forward.

Clodia gripped his neck, squeezing. "If you do not come, your lover will never be human again. And I will make sure Violetta and Tamuel pay too. I'm very good at curses, as you know. And I have the HeartsBlood Gem to help bind them." She tapped at the gem that was on a thick chain hanging around her neck.

"No. You can't." The ground pitched under her; her head still hazy from her vision.

"I can and I will, if you don't do as I say."

"How ... how do I know you will free him – free all of them – if I come like you ask? You broke your word last time. You cursed all of us."

"I was wrong. You aren't as stupid as Lianna." Clodia's slow smile made her shiver. "I vow on the life and power of our Goddess that I will not harm them if you come of your own free will. But if you do not come, all will die." She glanced at the clock. "You have an hour to decide." Then with another pop and displacement of air that pushed Jules against the wall, Clodia disappeared.

Jules scrabbled over the bed, grabbed her phone and stared at the date and time.

11:00 pm.

13 February.

Despair flooded her, stealing her breath.

She'd lost the day to her vision of Lianna and Sebastio.

"Why did you show me now?"

"You had to know. To know who Bastien is to us."

But she had known. Had always known. He was her

best friend, her constant companion and the one she loved as she loved no one else.

And he loved her. *Her*. Not because she was Lianna. He'd shown it in so many ways over the years, over the last few weeks, and she'd never seen it. Never been able to see it because of the curse. And her own self-doubt. But none of that mattered now – she loved him. She had to do anything to save him.

"*Hang on. Wait a minute. Why is there no pain?*"

"*Oh!*"

Her power. It hadn't punished her via the curse when Clodia had used Violetta's magic just now. Had it all been Clodia? No. She'd felt pain before coming here. Something else had changed – what? Did it even matter if it gave her an edge now?

She prodded at the power that had been locked inside her entire life. It flared under her touch – but not painfully so. Bright and strong, it leaped to life, making itself available for her command as if it had only been waiting for her to welcome it, to make herself open to it.

"*Goddess. I can feel our power!*"

"*Can you use it?*"

"*Can you?*"

"*I have no idea. I know the theory but I never got to use any of it myself.*"

"*Well, you better figure out how, because it's the only thing we've got going for us.*"

"*Not the only thing. You are so smart. I know you'll think of something.*"

Lianna was right. She might not know how to wrangle her power, but she'd spent most of her life reading about how others used their power. She could ... no, she *would* work something out. And if this was the last time she would ever have to use her power, she was going to make it count.

She could feel it now, coursing inside her, a spark quickly turning into a fire, a blaze. One she could not allow Clodia to have control over.

But how could she make certain of that and save Bastien, Tomaso and Violetta?

She had no time to figure it out. She just had to hope it would come to her. Disaster would reign if she didn't.

CHAPTER

TWENTY-TWO

J ules slowed as she approached the Colosseum, waiting for the barrage of visions to take her over, but nothing happened.

Clodia. It *had* all been Clodia's doing using Violetta's magic. How had none of them realised?

There had been little things that should have told her something was wrong with Violetta – little comments that stabbed at her confidence, a look she'd misinterpreted. Easy to not think it was something more nefarious given they were all under such stress – none of them had been behaving normally.

Clodia was so clever. So practiced with using magics. How could Jules ever think to beat her?

"No. No time for second guessing yourself now. I did that and look where it led me!"

She swallowed hard. *"You're right."* Stopping now wasn't an option even though she still didn't have a clue how to save her loved ones.

Her footsteps echoed against the ancient stone as she walked across the concourse and into the Forum. She'd

168

never seen it like this, her mind too full of visions of the past.

The ruins shone pale in the moonlight, the shadows shimmering with darkness. It should have been eerie, but it wasn't. It was just crumbling and sad – proof that even the strongest could falter and fall.

She straightened her shoulders as she picked her way across the ruins of the Temple of Vesta, to what had once been a lush private garden, and was now dirt and ruins and weeds. She came to a stop.

Clodia stood at the head of the pentacle Jules had unearthed two nights ago. Tomaso was there – no, not Tomaso. Tamuel. Her son!

"My son. We've found my son!"

Lianna pushed forward inside her, but she had to push back. They couldn't let any of that emotion in now. They had to keep their full wits about them.

She pushed the thought of their son away as she made herself take in the scene properly, looking for anything she could use.

Tamuel stood at the point he'd been placed in as a babe all those centuries ago, eyes and mouth open in horror, his body unmoving. She forced her gaze to move on from the pain of seeing him like that.

Where was Bastien?

There, on the ground, naked and glistening with sweat, body twitching from the magics of the change that had obviously just taken place.

"Bastien," she cried, racing towards him. His breath was shallow and his ribs showed clearly through his skin. He moaned as she touched him. "Shh, shh, I'm here."

His eyes flickered open, glowing in the night, the white giving way to stunning peridot – another sign the curse was weakening. But not gone. It still needed to be broken.

"Julianna." He reached up, hand trembling, to touch her face. "So beautiful."

"You can see me?"

"Yes."

She cupped his face, thumbs stroking across too sharp cheekbones.

He swallowed hard, eyes closing. "I'm so sorry. I couldn't stop her then and I can't stop her now. The gem is too strong."

"It's not your fault." She kissed his brow. "None of us could have known it was her. Here, I've brought you something to eat." She leaned back and pulled a chocolate bar from her jacket that she'd taken from the kitchen before she left. He reached for it, but his hands shook so badly, so she unwrapped it and held it to his lips, encouraging him to bite. It wouldn't be enough, but it was all she'd had time to get, hoping she would find him transformed by the time she got here.

He swallowed the first bite. "Thank you," he said on a grateful sigh.

"Enough." Clodia's voice snapped through the air. "It is almost time. Take your position."

"No," Bastien said, grabbing at her arm as she went to get to her feet. His grip was pathetically weak, but she stilled anyway as he whispered harshly, "Don't let her take your power. Save yourself."

She bent down and kissed him, lips lingering. "I will never leave you. Not again. Besides, I have to save Grand-mama – and our son."

"Our son?"

"Tamuel."

He gasped, gaze flickering to where Tamuel stood, trapped just like he was. "Of course – I should have seen it. There was something so familiar about him. I thought it was because he was a cupid, but it is because he looks a bit like his mother." His gaze returned to her. "If only I had some of my power. He and I could open a tear into the Heavenly plane and shove her where she should have gone long ag—" He jerked and cried out, face screwing up in pain, chocolate squishing in his fist.

"Bastien!"

"Leave him or I will increase his pain."

"Please, stop. I'll do as you ask." She scrambled to her feet.

Clodia smiled slowly, then lowered her hand. Bastien stopped writhing, but even though his muscles still twitched and he was covered in sweat, he looked up at her and whispered, "Don't do it."

"I love you," she whispered, then moved away to stand where Clodia told her to, where she remembered Lianna had given birth to their son. She looked across the pentacle at Tamuel. "I love you too," she said.

"I know, mother. I remember. I remember it all now. Do you?"

His voice – a youthful voice, not Tomaso's older one – rang in her head, his question capturing her mind.

Something clicked inside her. A rush of power surged, bringing with it knowledge, Lianna's and hers – learned but never used. She and Lianna might be the same, but they were also very different. And they'd learned different things about how to use magic. Where her knowledge faltered, Lianna's filled the gap. Just as where Lianna didn't know how to use what had not been practiced, Jules wasn't so constrained. She'd always known the strength of knowledge and how to use it.

And she knew exactly what to do with her powers to save those she loved.

That love, aided by the HeartsBlood Gem, had partially protected her in the past, stopping Clodia from reaching her goals. Love had chipped away at the bonds of the curse all these years; enough so that she was able to build a friendship with Bastien – loving him; enough that she loved and was loved by her grandmama and her parents; enough that she felt the connection with Tamuel even though she'd not understood it. It was enough to make her different from all those who'd come before.

Enough to give her the ability to use her unused power now because she finally understood its true strength.

And that love was even stronger now. It would be the thing that sent Clodia to hell.

She took her place in the pentacle. Clodia lifted her hands, the HeartsBlood Gem glowing on her chest. Jules almost laughed – Clodia had no idea what she was wearing. It was a part of Vesta. The essence of her power still lived inside it as it still lived inside Jules – that of home and hearth and fecundity and love – and it could never be used by someone who did not understand. It was a power that would never properly bend to Clodia's will.

It would destroy her.

"*Are you sure about this?*"

"*Hells yeah. If Clodia wants our power, she can have it. All of it.*"

"Jules, no!"

Bastien pushed himself to his knees, arm stretched out towards her, the light of life in him horribly dimmed. The darkness of Clodia's power twined around him already –

she would never keep her word. She was going to sap him and Tamuel and Violetta of power to do this thing.

Jules wouldn't let her. "Trust me?"

"You can't give her your power. Not to save me."

"Or me," Tamuel said in her head.

"Trust me," she said to both of them.

They both nodded wildly. "I do. Always."

"As do I." The words echoed doubly in her mind, Tamuel's voice combined with Lianna's.

It was all she needed. She turned back to Clodia. The ancient witch had finished her spell, ready to release it. She sucked power from Bastien and Tamuel and from the fifth, empty point – a link to the Eternal Well? Even better. The Gods and Goddesses would not like what Clodia was doing. "I'm ready," she said, her voice calm.

"Open yourself to me, girl, so I can break the curse and begin the transfer," Clodia shouted. "Let me have what should have been mine. Now."

Clodia's dark power darted towards her. An intense pressure then a breaking pop in her head as the curse broke. She had no time to breathe in relief as more dark power was sent her way, this time intent on draining Jules' power slowly, painfully.

Jules had other ideas. She lifted her hands. Power shot through her, sparking out of her fingers, lighting the night, arrowing to Clodia in an almighty burst.

The night lit up with the brightness of the sun as the power hit the HeartsBlood Gem then shot into Clodia, amplified.

The witch screamed. "No, no, it's too much. Slow down. I can't take it all at once."

"You wanted it all," Jules said, grinning. "You can have it." She concentrated harder, sending more power through the conduit Clodia had unwisely opened, allowing Jules access to the naked, dark heart of her. That heart was strong. Weakened, but not destroyed yet.

She'd have to use all her power.

She shoved power and more power at the bitch-witch. Clodia screamed, the sound a shrieking echo of rage and terror.

"Jules, not all of it." Tamuel's shout reached her – she'd freed him and Bastien with her action – and they had raced across the pentacle to her side.

"It has to be nearly all," she whispered, then pushed every last ounce of what was inside her out and into Clodia. "It is the only way to be truly rid of her."

The blast of power had the effect she wanted – it shoved the spirit out of Violetta. Her grandmama collapsed onto the earth, unconscious – but it wasn't quite enough. Clodia was diminished but still there, her ghostly figure hanging above Violetta's body, trying desperately to reach her again – the only way she could now survive was in a living body.

"A tear. We need to shove her where she'll never bother us again," Jules gasped. She had used nearly all her power and didn't have enough to finish the job herself.

Bastien and Tamuel put their hands on her shoulders and opened themselves to her. Such love. Such trust.

She took their power and bound it with the remaining remnants of her power and her own love and trust for them. "I forgive you, Clodia," she said. "But I don't think the Gods will. They don't like it when people have the hubris to steal their power. Tamuel, now."

He shoved power into her – such incredible power – and she tore open a fissure into the realms of the Gods, and with more of her power, bolstered by Bastien's, Jules shoved Clodia through the tear.

Clodia's scream disappeared into the shimmering grey beyond the tear, but it didn't close. It pulsed then she felt something tug at her.

Gods! The Void wanted more – it wanted all the power that had torn a hole in it.

It tugged at her again, pulling her across the pentacle.

"Fight it!" Bastien, Tamuel and Lianna all yelled.

But she couldn't. She saw the fingers of darkness from within – the remnants of Clodia's dark powers or something else? – reaching out, seeking, heading towards her love and her son.

"No!" she cried, shoving what remained of her power at the tear so that it caught at the darkness then flew into the Void.

The tear shimmered, warped then closed with a whoosh.

Wind whipped up, wiping away the last embers of the pentacle.

Silence fell.

Her knees buckled.

Her lover and her son caught her and carried her over to sit on a flat stone. Despite the chill in the air, the stone was warmed from the magic that had burned the air only moments ago.

Magic powered by a love that had lasted through the ages.

Bastien came down before her, clothing himself as he did, his gaze full of love and yet tinged by sadness. "Jules. Your power. You sent all your power into the Void with her. Why did you do that?"

"It was the only way," she said, wishing he'd stop

talking and just kiss her. "Didn't you feel it? There was something coming out of the Void – Clodia or something. I had to close the tear before she – or it – could take a hold. It wanted my power so I gave all of it. It was the only way to save us all."

"My love." He stroked her face, his eyes full of loss. "I'm so sorry."

"It's okay. I'm okay."

"How did you know to do that?"

She looked up at Tamuel. "I read about it."

He gaped at her. Bastien chuckled. "Of course you did."

"And Bastien – do I call you Bastien? Or would you prefer Sebastio?"

"I'm Bastien for you. Your Bas."

Her smile felt like it took up her entire face. "Bas gave me the idea about sending her through to a place only the Gods have access to." She smiled at her love, staring into his peridot eyes. "So beautiful. I'm so glad I finally get to see these and not just dream about them."

He took her hand and kissed her knuckles. "I would give up my sight if it meant you could have your magic back."

"I wouldn't." She cupped his cheek, making him meet her gaze. "Why do I need it? I have my work. I have you. And now I also have a son." She reached out her free hand to Tamuel. He took her hand in his, holding it to his chest. She smiled up at him then back at Bastien. "It's all I've ever wanted. All I've ever wished for." She looked back at her hand wrapped in Tamuel's. "And I can touch you without worrying how it will affect me. That is magic enough."

"So wise," Tamuel said, then shimmered, his suave older man form changing into that of a young man, with twinkling eyes that flashed to peridot for a moment before settling to a beautiful indigo, and hair as darkly auburn and curling as hers. He squeezed her hand, his smile blazing brightly enough to light the night. "You may not be the mother that birthed me, but you're the mother of my heart."

"My son. Tell him I love him."

She did just that, brushing away the tears that leaked from the corners of his eyes.

Bastien put his hand on Tamuel's shoulder. "Son. Why did you never tell me who you were?"

"It was forbidden. To keep me from being swept into Clodia's curse, Eros took me from the pentacle in the confusion after Clodia's spell went awry. He wanted to take you too, but you were bound in ways I wasn't. So, he hid me and gave me to Persephone until it was time for me to become one of his cupids. She told me of you and what had happened and helped me look for ways to break the curse's hold on you both. She followed Esta, thinking she was a key and rescued her journal from the house fire all those years ago. She kept that fact hidden from me and only left clues so I could find it just recently. When it became clear that now was the time to use it. That you," he turned his gaze to Jules, "were the one who could break the spell."

"So in a way, my father did help me."

"I suppose he did given he gave me to the one Goddess who might help. I'm so sorry though."

"For what?"

"That it took so long to be able to help you. Until a century ago, I was forbidden to contact you."

Bastien cupped Tamuel's cheek. "That is not your fault, son. The Gods and Goddesses do things for their own purposes. You were bound as much as Jules and I."

"But I almost blew it tonight. Persephone mentioned that Clodia's spirit might still be hanging around the place of her greatest defeat, but I didn't remember the warning until it was too late. I let her take the Hearts-Blood Gem from me because I was too prideful, too stupid."

"No. You trusted," Jules said. "Don't ever feel sorry for that."

"Mother," he said, tears in his eyes. "I am sorry. So sorry the ultimate sacrifice was your magic."

Jules touched his cheek. "I'm just glad the sacrifice wasn't this." She cupped his cheek with one hand, Bastien's with the other. "Clodia thought my magic the most valuable thing, but it wasn't. This is. So don't be sad. Not when we've finally found each other."

A moan from the other side of the cleared area had her pushing to her feet. "Oh Goddess! Grandmama," Jules cried, rushing over to where Violetta had fallen. She couldn't believe she'd forgotten her grandmama was still there.

Violetta looked up at her, her eyes shadowed as Jules reached her. "You did it, my girl."

"I did."

"Your magic?"

"Gone. I had to use it all to defeat Clodia and close the rip into the Void."

Violetta sighed and nodded. "I am sorry."

"I'm not."

Violetta nodded, her gaze skating over Jules' smile. "Bastien and Tomaso – I mean, Tamuel?"

"Here," they both said, then helped her up.

She trembled, her form thinner than it had been before – Clodia had pulled a lot out of her in the possession and final spell. She pulled the HeartsBlood Gem from around her neck. "Here, this is yours." She held it out to Jules.

"No, I—"

"As a reminder of the strength you showed tonight and of what truly matters."

Jules took the gem and hung it around her neck. It pulsed warmly there, feeling like it belonged. "Let's go home."

"Let me," Bastien said. "I haven't been able to use my true powers for 2000 years." He waved his hand. The air shimmered around them and then they were in the *pensione's* kitchen.

Jules held still, waiting for the nausea and pain, but it didn't come.

She was finally free.

She hugged Bastien to her as Tamuel helped Violetta to a seat, put the kettle on and began to raid the fridge.

Bastien hugged her back, his smile warming her like the sun. "Jules. You know I will never leave you. You have no need to doubt that."

"I know. I understand now. You're *my* love. Forever."

"Forever together, *my* love." His lips met hers and everything faded as she lost herself in Bastien's touch, in his kiss, and it was better than anything she could ever have wished. Love cursed no more. She was love blessed.

In the distance, church bells tolled one am. Tamuel glanced over at his mother and father, then, mouth quirking in happiness, put a plate of meat, cheese and bread in front of Violetta. "It's Valentine's Day," he said.

"Yes." She glanced over at Jules and Bastien, lost to everything else in the joy of their kiss. "It seems fitting."

"I'm going to find some way to get her power back to her."

Violetta's smile grew wide as she picked up a piece of

cheese. "That would be nice. Although, I don't think she needs it to make her happy. Not now she finally knows the man of her dreams."

"The man of her reality," Tamuel countered.

Violetta winked at him. "May we all be blessed with such a reality."

Tamuel nodded but didn't say anything further.

Nobody could know he planned to bargain anything – even his greatest power – for his mother's magic. The power of a cupid. It was one of the most sought-after powers among the Gods because what was stronger than love? Look at what it had done here tonight.

Jules deserved to be the witch she was born to be. Not just to have magic, but to have true immortality. His mother and father deserved to be together forever.

And he was the cupid who was going to make it happen. He vowed it.

A rumble in the distance signalled the Eternal Well had accepted his vow.

He smiled.

💗 THE END 💗

...

OR IS IT?

❥

IF YOU ENJOYED BAS AND JULES' fated mates, second chance romance and want more, then you're going to love this. Because I wrote a thing ... a hot, sexy thing ...

An NSFW love scene (2 whole chapters worth!) for Bas and Jules that follows on directly from the ending you've just read.

It is a scene that Bas and Jules have been begging me to write for ages and so I finally gave in (yeah, I didn't need my arm twisted too badly!)

But, before we get to that, I want to share the first chapter of the next book in the series with you. Because I know if you enjoyed Jules and Bas' story, then you're going to love Tamuel and Korinna's story in **Soul Cursed: Gods Cursed Series Book 2.**

Read on for a sneak peek at the first chapter of **Soul Cursed**:

SOUL CURSED

GODS CURSED SERIES BOOK 2

TAMUEL'S CURSE

"You cannot kill this child, witch, for he belongs to me. Of my flesh, I am the only one with the authority to take his life. But as you point out, the Gods' laws dictate that the son will pay for the hubris of the father. I will curse this child's soul, not for your purposes, Clodia, but for mine!

Hear me this day: I bind this child to my service, to be bound more tightly than any other cupid by his cupid powers. He will find love for others in his service, but is never to seek it for himself. Only the cracked piece of his soul's mirror, cursed both equal and opposite, will make him whole and set him free."

Eros to Vestal Priestess-Witch Clodia: as etched into the holy Keeper of the Curses, Revenant of the Eternal Well.

CHAPTER
ONE

Tamuel stumbled on the smooth black floor as the portal closed with a little whoosh behind him. He quickly steadied himself, blinked then glanced down at the chronometer on his wrist. The ancient clockwork dial glowed as it whirred silently. Not too bad. The time difference between the Underworld and the Earthly Realm hadn't shrunk too much as the veil thinned for All Hallows' Eve. He took a breath – time to get on with his quest. It wouldn't do to get caught here.

He looked around, orienting himself. This wasn't quite what he expected the tunnels of the Underworld to look like, but then again, what would he know? It wasn't like there were tourist brochures. Perhaps there should be though. The veins of red, purple and green that ran chaotically along the glossy black rock walls, lighting the space, were quite pretty.

But why was it so warm? He didn't think this part of the Underworld was supposed to have the Fires of Hell – that was a particular quirk only found in the Morningstar's kingdom. Damn – had the portal dumped him in the wrong part of the Hell Realms?

He turned then stilled. He wasn't in tunnels – he stood in what looked like a large lounge room complete with spring-green rug, red upholstered furniture and flowers on every buffet, side table and antique drawers scattered around the room.

Standing in front of a fireplace that looked like it had been hewn by giant teeth, limned by the flickering firelight, were a couple in a lover's embrace.

Not just any couple. Hades and Persephone.

Shit-fuck-damn! What in all the hells were they doing here? They were supposed to be at Persephone's All Hallows' Eve party.

He must have done something wrong. His spell was supposed to have dropped him right outside Varagustus' cell. It sure as damnation wasn't supposed to drop him into Hades' private lounge room.

This was not at all going to plan.

Thank all the Gods neither Hades nor Persephone noticed him portal in uninvited. Famous for their displays of PDA, they were currently too wrapped up in their kiss – and in a state of half-undress – to notice him standing near the door. Actually, only Hades was partly undressed. Persephone was obviously in costume for her Halloween party. A quick glance at the broken horns, trident and torn cape that lay on the green rug in front of Hades' throne-like armchair had Tamuel guessing it was the reason they were still here. Hades famously hated dressing up.

What a bloody cock-up! He hadn't taken Hades' mood into consideration when planning this. The Fates must be meddling again – they loved pulling on unexpected threads and watching the chaos that unfolded. He was certain they did it for shits and giggles. He wished there was a way to show them just how not funny their meddling was.

He glanced at his bloody right wrist where the sigil for the portal spell was carved into his skin. Hades and Persephone still being here could ruin everything. He had to find Clodia and get her to tell him what she'd done with his mother's powers. He'd made a vow and it was either succeed or die trying.

He'd prefer the dying part didn't happen now though.

He backed up, hoping to reach the open door behind him before they finished kissing. This could still work as long as he could get out of here before they noticed him.

He was almost at the door when Persephone muttered, "Please, my hell beast. I'll let you suck on my toes if you put on the Lucifer costume."

"But you don't like it when I do that, honey-flower."

"But you like it, my sexy-wexy-lover-boy. And while you do that, I'll suck your c—"

"'Ew -ew." TMI even for a cupid. Tamuel skittered backwards, desperate to get out of the room before he saw something he'd never be able to forget. He turned ... and bounced off Hades' naked chest.

Damn you Fates. He'd obviously made enough noise to catch the God of the Underworld's attention. Rallying – and trying to ignore the God's raging hard-on that tented his jeans – he smiled up at Hades. "Happy All Hallows' Eve, Uncle."

Hades didn't smile. "I don't remember receiving notice from Eros that one of his cupids was coming down for a visit," he said smoothly, turning back to look at his wife. "Do you remember asking Eros to send one of his cupids down here, my passion flower?"

Persephone crossed her arms, shaking her head a little.

"No, I did not, pooky-wooky. What are you doing here, Tamuel?"

"Well, I—"

"I smell blood." Hades' gaze snapped to the blood dripping on the floor then at its source – the sigil carved into Tamuel's skin.

He made to back away, but Hades grabbed Tamuel by the wrist, lifting it to his nose. He sniffed at the bloody sigil then, black eyes flaring red as they met Tamuel's, he snarled, "You're corporeal. Who showed you that magic, boy?"

Shit. Shit. This so wasn't going how he'd planned – slip in, find Varagustus, get the information he wanted, steal a Hells-Key, travel to Tartarus and question Clodia, then back out before Hades even knew he'd come here. But there was no point lying to the angry God standing before him. Hiding his wince of pain as the God of the Underworld's fingers tightened around his wrist, he said, "Nobody, Uncle. I found it."

Hades growled, fingers tightening further – pain slashed through Tamuel as something snapped in his wrist. Hades' grip tightened as he barked out, "I don't believe you. Zeus and I made Persephone and Demeter rid the world of this heresy many centuries past." He leaned in closer, a growl in his throat, black eyes flashing orange then red. "Tell me who told you of this spell."

The God jerked his hand; something else snapped. Lights sparked before Tamuel's eyes and he almost went to his knees.

"Well?" Hades shook him.

Tears stinging his eyes, Tamuel managed to say, "I've always been ... interested ... in ... the Eleusinian Mysteries. I found ... writings on them."

"Impossible," Persephone said, coming forward to stand beside Hades. She might be pixie-like to her husband's towering brute, but in that moment, she was the far more frightening. "Who betrayed us?"

"I—" His mind whirled, trying to come up with something, anything, but the pain as Hades crushed his wrist made that impossible. Darkness whirled around him and he ...

Shaking brought him back to consciousness; pain spiked through him, the warmth of blood running down his arm – his suit was going to be ruined, he thought groggily. Someone was yelling something. More shaking and pain brought his attention back to the God still holding him up by his mangled wrist. "Wha?" he slurred.

"Tell us, cupid, or your body and your spirit won't leave the Underworld this All Hallows' Eve – or ever again."

Despite the danger and threat, Hades' beautiful voice coiled around Tamuel, drawing him in, making it impossible to deny him what he wanted, no matter how he'd promised not to tell on ... "Demeter."

"My mother?" Persephone said.

He nodded, then cried out again as Hades squeezed and broken bones ground together. Darkness threatened to take him down once more. "Please, my lord," he gasped. "My wrist. You're crushing ... it."

"Ease up, pumpkin pie. You don't want him to pass out before he tells you what we want to know."

"Whatever you say, honey bunny." He let go.

Tamuel dropped to the floor. He knew he shouldn't take his eyes off Hades, but couldn't help looking down at his shattered wrist. He almost fainted at the sight. But it wasn't so much the bones that poked through his skin that made him break into a cold sweat: the sigil was destroyed. He hadn't memorised it; had hoped to copy it from one wrist to the other for his return but now ...

"Oh Hades, look what you've done."

"It's no more than he deserves for using that spell."

Hades tapped his foot. Tamuel looked up at him, mind whirring, his thoughts clearer now that Hades had stopped inflicting pain. Eros had spent hours lecturing him when he was younger about the importance of dealing with what came next rather than what came after. He really wished he'd listened because if he didn't find some way of getting Hades and Persephone to understand, then there was no point in worrying if he could remember the sigil or not: he wasn't making it out of this room alive.

Trying to ignore the sick throbbing pain in his wrist and arm – and the fear he maybe had finally bitten off more than he could chew – he pushed to his feet, straightened his shoulders and met the God of the Underworld's angry gaze. He'd already broken his promise, so ... "Demeter gave it into my keeping centuries ago."

"She wouldn't do that," Persephone said, delicate features filled with hurt and anger.

"She did."

"But we destroyed all the words together. Wiped all the followers' minds."

"Not all. She couldn't do that to her favourite priestess, Carianthe. She hid her from you and let her keep her memories. Carianthe wrote her life's work all over again in the last years of her life. After she died, Demeter couldn't bring herself to destroy it, so she gave it to me to hide with the other treasures I had in my keeping."

"Your mother," Hades snarled at Persephone. "I should have known she'd find some way of screwing this up. I just never thought she hated me so much that she'd risk this. Wait until I get my hands on her ... I'll—"

"You'll do nothing to my mother," Persephone said, grabbing her husband's hands as they made a wringing motion. "I will take her to task over this. But first, we must find out why Mum gave Tamuel a copy of the Eleusinian Mysteries Grimoire. Did she want you to use this spell?"

Hades turned to him, fire in his eyes. "Did she?" He grabbed Tamuel's wrist, pulling him up by it. "Did she?"

He clamped down on the scream, forcing himself to hold onto consciousness – he'd never seen his uncle this angry before. Didn't want to think what might happen if he passed out. "No," he ground out through clenched teeth, pain a writhing thing inside him. "She just wanted me ... to keep it safe ... in memory of her ... beloved priestess."

"Why did you look at it then?"

"Your mother said ... I might have use of ... certain spells one day ... when I was desperate. She said I was only to ... look at it then ... I would know when. Please, Uncle. My wrist."

Hades pulled him closer. "Did you tell anyone of it?"

"No!" Well, except for the ghost who had helped him realise what the spell was. But Hades didn't need to know about that. He met the God's angry gaze as he said earnestly, "I would never ... give this spell to anyone else. Never."

Hades stared him down for long moments, eyes sparking.

Gods, was he going to kill him? His uncle had always been kind to him. Much kinder than all the other Gods. Probably helped by the fact that Persephone had taken him under her wing for a while when he'd been a youth, allowing him to be trained alongside her Soteira at the

Amazonian and Gargarean warrior training camp; something no other cupid before or since had been allowed to do.

"Silly boy," Persephone tutted. "What did you think was going to happen when you were caught with this spell on your arm? You have to know it not only allows someone in and out of the Underworld in corporeal form, but allows a spirit to gain a body and use it to escape?"

"You weren't supposed ... to be here."

She shook her head at him. "My fondness for you may not be enough to get you out of trouble this time." She brushed her hand down the side of his face, frowning. "I really was hoping to get to my party on time this year."

He looked at her, desperately. "I had no choice. I made a vow."

"The Eternal Well accepted?"

"Yes," Tamuel grated.

She gasped, glancing at Hades. "This is what made you break one of our most sacred laws?"

"I need to speak to ... one of your guests," Tamuel panted, spots still sparking in front of his eyes. "I just need ... information ... to get my mother's power back."

A look flashed between Hades and Persephone before she said, "Enough, Hades. We need to hear what the boy has to say." The Goddess put her arm around Tamuel. "He doesn't deserve to be punished for what is obviously one of my mother's meddling visions."

"But that spell—"

"I'm sorry I ... used it ... I just ... want to get my mother's ... powers back to her. Without them, she'll only have ... a human life. I can't lose her ... or my father ... again. I just can't." He swallowed hard against pain of a different sort

194

that thickened his throat. "Besides ... they deserve ... a true happy ever after. Like you have."

Hades shared a look with Persephone that made something in Tamuel's chest tighten, then suddenly let go his grip. Tamuel almost wept in relief as he clutched his broken arm to his chest, thankful Persephone was there to hold him up – despite her diminutive size, she was very strong.

"I wish I could help you with your parents' plight," Hades said quietly. "But I do not have your mother's powers, boy."

Tamuel took a few long, deep breaths, finally managing to push the pain aside as he'd been taught to do – at least enough for him to say steadily, "I know. But that witch-bitch Clodia does. And I know she's here. I know that you and Zeus tracked her down in the Void and imprisoned her in Tartarus for her hubris in stealing my mother's Goddess-given powers."

"I shoved her in a cell myself and set her punishment. But the power you say she stole is no longer in her."

He'd heard that too. "I want to ask her what happened to it," he said as Persephone began to shepherd him towards the couch.

"Given the fact she didn't tell me, no matter how much I tortured her, what makes you think she will tell you?"

"Because I have this." He pulled on the chain that hung around his neck, lifting it until the HeartsBlood Gem popped out from his shirt to swing in front of him. "Clodia tied her soul to this. With the right spell, I can compel her to answer my questions using the power the gem has over her."

Persephone lowered him to the couch. "This is the reason you decided to use that spell?"

"The only way to bring it here was if I was in corporeal

form. It's the only thing that will get Clodia to talk. But ... It won't work for me. I was hoping to speak to Varagustus first – the spell was supposed to take me to his cell."

"Varagustus?" Persephone shared another look with Hades. "Why Varagustus?"

"His knowledge of magical gems is greater than any before or after him. But I think he held a lot of knowledge back from his writings. I'm certain he will know what I need to do to use the gem."

Persephone looked up at her husband. "Hades ..."

"No good will come of it."

"It's what we've been waiting for," Persephone said, her hand on Hades' arm as she looked up into his eyes. "She's only gotten worse. She's not been anywhere for centuries. I had no idea when I agreed ..."

"Don't blame yourself for that, my blooming rose."

Persephone shook her head. "What matters blame if she's intrigued enough by this? Especially with the Hearts-Blood Gem in play. What if this is the true reason my mother sent him down here? She has always felt guilty about what happened. About the choices we all made. Please, honey-bee."

"But you know how our guest feels. I wouldn't want to force her, my spring's delight."

"It isn't your choice, bunny-wunny."

"Her who?" Tamuel asked.

They didn't answer, just had a staring match.

Finally, Hades threw his hands up, sighing gustily as he turned back to Tamuel. "Fine. Say I do agree to you travelling to Tartarus—"

"You will," Persephone said, beaming at him. He glared at her but she waved her hand at him as she took a seat next to Tamuel. "If for no other reason than you and your siblings do not wish that power to stay wherever it is. It unbalances things. It should be with the witch it was intended for – Tamuel's mother."

"So, you'll help me?" He couldn't believe his luck in this turnaround. He had no idea giving up Demeter would lead to this – he'd deal with her anger later. Right now, he wasn't going to look a gift horse in the mouth. Not even what could be a Trojan one.

Hades nodded begrudgingly. "I will. But there are three issues. The first being, I will not let you anywhere in my kingdom with that spell etched on your arm for anyone to see. Persephone can heal your wrist, but that sigil will not be left intact. You will need to remember it, only carving its mirror into your other wrist just before you wish to travel back."

Tamuel swallowed hard. "Not a problem." He hoped. He just needed a moment to sit down and go into his memory vault and retrieve it.

Hades nodded. "The second is the matter of the ticking clock. If you don't mirror that spell work and get back through the portal by the time the clock strikes twelve in the Earthly Realm on All Hallows' Eve, your soul *will* be cursed to stay trapped down here forever."

He opened his mouth to say it wouldn't be a problem, but Persephone raised her hand, her voice echoing strangely as she said, "The veil is thinning and time is constantly changing. This year more than any others. The current alignment of the stars heralds dark portents that place a shadow over all the Realms." She blinked and swallowed hard. "It is not a good time to travel through the Underworld, especially for a corporeal being."

He didn't like the sound of that. Not that it mattered – it was now or never. "Lucky I'm wearing this then." He gestured to the chronometer. If it worked as it should, it would tell him how the time shifted and warn him of changes in relation to the Earthly Realm – no matter what the stars heralded with their eerie portents. "I should be out of here well in time, even if the weeks I currently have turn to days. As long as I can have a Hells-Key?"

Hades' brow lowered. Persephone coughed. They glared at each other, making Tamuel wish he could read minds because he was certain there was quite the conversation going on.

Finally, Hades rolled his eyes. "I will give you a Hells-Key to move around the Underworld with more ease. But there is one last sticking point, one I have no say over."

"And what is that?"

"Varagustus didn't write those treatises on gems. The woman who did is not one of my prisoners."

"What? But if I can't find out how to use the gem, then my trip here is pointless."

Hades raised his hand. "She is not a prisoner. She is a valued member of my household. And she has refused to see anyone for centuries – aside from us, the servants and those she wants to interview of course."

"I will do whatever it takes to make her agree to help me."

"She may want the HeartsBlood Gem in payment," Persephone said.

He glanced down at the gem hanging around his neck. It wasn't his to give but ... "Fine. I cannot go home empty-handed."

Hades and Persephone shared a look again before she said, "Then I will take you to her. But first, I will heal your arm – Korinna doesn't like the sight of blood."

"Korinna?" His mouth dried. "You don't mean Korinna Soteira?"

"The very one." Persephone shot him a brief, sad smile as she began the healing.

Korinna Soteira. The name rang in his head, his thoughts too lost to the past to truly feel the pain of the healing as it burned through his skin and bones.

Korinna had not only broken his heart but had crushed it under her dainty foot almost two thousand years ago. The rejection had left him bleeding and wishing for death.

But none of that mattered now. All that mattered was his vow. "Take me to her. I'm sure she will speak to me."

She owed him that at least.

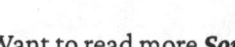

Want to read more *Soul Cursed*?
Get your copy here:

https://books2read.com/u/38OvOL

BEFORE YOU GO, I want to get back to what I mentioned before - something a little extra special (and a lot sexy) for you. Just turn the page ...

WANT TO READ A LITTLE SOMETHING SEXY?

YOUR BONUS NSFW SCENES ARE WAITING

GET YOUR EXCLUSIVE BONUS NSFW EPILOGUE TO LOVE CURSED RIGHT HERE:

Yes! I have written a bonus NSFW sex-scene for Bas and Jules. It takes place just after the events of *Love Cursed.* And it was soo full on I and so hot I couldn't wrap it up in 1 chapter - I had to write 2!

But how do you get your hands on these hot-hot chapters I hear you ask? That's easy! Just follow the QR code, fill in your details and the chapters will be winging their way to you soon after.

Before you go, if you've got a moment, I would love it if you could leave a review for *Love Cursed*. Reviews can help readers find books, and also help tell me where I'm going right and where I'm going wrong. I am grateful for all honest reviews. Thank you in advance for taking the time to let others know what you've read, and what you thought—you can leave your review at Goodreads, BookBub or the ebook retailer where you bought your copy. You can find links to the ebook retailers here:

https://www.leislleighton.com/paranormal-romance-novels/#LoveCursed

But wait! There's more ...

If you're not into newsletters but think you might be into subscriptions that give you serialised content, exclusive chapters to new books, exclusive bonus content, signed print books and much more, then turn the page to find out about Leisl's Legends - you can also get the NSFW Bonus love scene for Jules and Bas there as well.

Read on ...

JOIN LEISL'S LEGENDS

Subscribe to (or follow) me (via the QR code) at my Leisl's Legends page on REAM—a new subscription app like Patreon except it's designed especially for readers and authors for an amazing reading experience— and you will get early access to *The Huntress and the Vampire*  *King*, my hot enemies to lovers, witch-and-vampire-licious urban fantasy romance that readers over there are already in love with. It's the prequel novel to the first book in the Blood-Rites Series - *The Blood of the Seer*. Be the first to find out where it all began with Anita and Hei's love story.

You will also get exclusive early access to the next book

in the **Gods Cursed Series** and can comment on the story as I write it! Your feedback could be essential in shaping the next book in the series.

Be part of creating the stories you love AND get exclusive access to a whole range of goodies including other WIPs, bonus content, voting rights, signed books and much, much more.

BECOME A LEGEND NOW!
https://reamstories.com/leislleightonauthor

THE HUNTRESS AND THE VAMPIRE KING

She hates the vampire who saved her; he holds the key to her fate ...

Hunter-witch Anita Middleton wants revenge against the violent vampire cults that murdered her father and has worked hard to become one of the best vampire hunters there is. But on a difficult hunt she is caught in an ambush and is mortally wounded ... only to be saved by a mysterious warrior. A warrior with brilliant blue eyes and long silver-blonde hair who fights with a grace and violence like nothing she's seen. It is only after she wakes in the heart of his palazzo that she realises her saviour is a vampire - and according to her brother and mentor, this vampire king is their ally.

Lord Hei rules over an empire of witches, humans and vampires who have been trying to keep the vicious vampire cults, the Wild and Dark Brethren, at bay for centuries. Then he saves Anita and knows with one look she is the prophecied Huntress who could be his downfall or his salvation - and she is also his fated mate. But she struggles to trust him as her hatred of vampires is deep-seated. And she *needs* to trust him because only he can offer the specialised training a Huntress needs so her power won't overwhelm her.

But with the Dark Brethren mysteriously amassing, he has little time to win her over. And Anita must go on a crash course to learn how to control her Huntress magic ... or go slowly and violently insane.

The Huntress and the Vampire King is the exciting action-packed prequel novel to *The Blood of the Seer*.

If you love your vampires hot with a bit of The Witcher thrown in and your heroines as kick-arse as Buffy and even more tortured, if you love fated mates, enemies to lovers, chosen ones and epically hot  **romance mixed with action and mystery, then** *The Huntress and the Vampire King* **is what you've been waiting for.**

Sign up to Leisl's Legends (via the QR code above) and start reading exclusive early release chapters of it now!

Also by Leisl Leighton

Gods Cursed Series

A Love Cursed Christmas Wish

Love Cursed

Soul Cursed

Blood Cursed

Hearts Cursed

Fates Cursed

Witch Cursed

Dragon Cursed

(Coming 2026)

Blood-Rites Series

The Blood of the Seer

The Blood of the Sire

The Blood of the Son

(Coming 2027)

Blood-Rites Prequel and Bonus Material

The Huntress and the Vampire King

The Middleton Manifesto

(Available now via Leisl's Legends subscription)

~

PACK BOUND SERIES

Pack Bound

Moon Bound

Shifter Bound

Wolf Bound

Witch Bound

(A Pack Bound Series Prequel Novella)

BOX SET

Pack Bound Series Collection Books 1-4

~

DAWN OF THE CURSE

A PACK BOUND PREQUEL SERIES

Soul Bound

Alpha Bound

Hunter Bound

Fae Bound

(Coming in 2027)

~

ANTHOLOGIES

A Perfectly Paranormal Valentine

A Perfectly Paranormal Halloween

A Perfectly Paranormal Easter

A Perfectly Paranormal Christmas

A Perfectly Paranormal Prophecy

(Coming in 2027)

～

As well as writing sexy, epic and romantic paranormal novels, I write mysterious and emotional romantic suspense novels too. Check out the following titles for amazing, suspenseful reads:

STORM HAVEN SERIES

Need You Tonight

The Devil Inside

～

COALCLIFF STUD SERIES

Climbing Fear: Book 1

Blazing Fear: Book 2

～

ECHO SPRINGS SERIES

Dangerous Echoes: Book 1

Books 2-4 in this series, (written by Daniel deLorne, TJ Hamilton and Shannon Curtis) are also available now at all ebook retailers.

About Leisl

Leisl Leighton is a tall red head with an overly large imagination. As a child, she identified strongly with Anne of Green Gables, and like Anne, is a voracious reader and born performer.

It came as no surprise when she went on to a career as a performer, script writer, script doctor, stage manager and musical director for cabaret and theatre restaurants.

After starting a family, Leisl stopped performing and began writing the stories plaguing her dreams. She now writes emotional stories mixed with mystery and a little bit of what goes bump in the night.

Her novels have won and placed in writing contests here and overseas. She is a passionate advocate for the romance genre, was President of Romance Writers of Australia from 2014-2017 and when she's not writing romantic stories of  redemption, she is helping other authors reach their dreams with her Author Services. You can contact Leisl through her website via the QR Code above or here: https://www.leislleighton.com

And if you want to stay in touch and be the first to find out about new releases, appearances, special deals and exclusive content and giveaways, sign up to her Newsletter and pick up your free copy of *Fractured Curse* via the QR code.

Or sign up to *Leisl's Legends* via this QR code to get *Fractured Curse* plus serialised early access stories and bonus content including a bonus NSFW ending for Love Cursed.

You can also follow her on social media:

 facebook.com/LeislLeightonAuthor

 instagram.com/leislleightonauthor

 bookbub.com/authors/leisl-leighton

 amazon.com/stores/Leisl-Leighton/author/B00DBYRGZY

ACKNOWLEDGMENTS

Thanks go to all the usual people: my hubby (the love of my life) and my boys (the other loves of my life); my mum and dad; my sister, brother and their families; my writing group friends—Anita, Marnie, Chris, Laura, Frana—I could do none of this without your love and support through the good and bad (especially in this last few terrible years). You give me the strength to keep going and the room to keep filling my creative well.

Thanks to Helen and Liz—your counsel and amazing friendships will always be missed but what you brought to my life will never be forgotten

Thanks to my agent, Alex Adsett, for encouraging me to go off and pursue getting these stories out there myself.

Thanks once again to my editor, Marnie St Clair—working with you is always a joy.

Thanks to Samantha Marshall for your amazing cover.

And a big thanks to my fellow A Perfectly Paranormal writers – this would not have been written without you. I'll be eternally grateful that you thought of me when coming up with the idea for the anthologies for which this series idea was spawned. It is exciting that this story will live on both in the anthology but also as its own little can-do novel.

Finally, thanks to all the readers. I love writing my stories but it makes it all the more special to know you're right there with me enjoying my characters' trials, joys and general shenanigans right along with me. I hope my stories lift you up and give you all the feels because then my job is done.